EVERY LOVE STORY HAS TWO SIDES

POLLY'S STORY . . .

I seemed to be spending a lot of time looking out windows at boys. That was my life—look, but don't touch. A parade of boys went through our house every week, but for all they noticed me, they might as well have been on a movie screen.

Polly's fourteen going on fifteen, and she's a little tired of always being treated like a kid by her brother, Pearce, and his gang of handsome friends. Can't they see that she's almost as grown-up as the girls they date? Even Mac, the only one of Pearce's friends who's nice to her, still treats her like a little girl. That is, until they both find themselves away from home for the summer at Silver Beach. Suddenly Mac needs a friend, someone to talk to, someone to spend the summer with. And Polly is right there.

TWO BY TWO ROMANCES™ are designed to show you both sides of each special love story in this series. You get two complete books in one. Read what it's like for a girl to fall in love. Then turn the book over and find out what love means to the boy.

Polly's story begins on page one of this half of *One Special Summer*. Does Mac feel the same way? Flip the book over and read his story to find out.

You'll Want to Read All the Books in the
TWO BY TWO ROMANCE™ Series

5

TWO BY TWO
ROMANCE™

One Special Summer

Janice Harrell

WARNER BOOKS

A Warner Communications Company

Two By Two Romance™ is a *trademark of Riverview Books, Inc.*

First Warner Books Printing: March, 1984

10 9 8 7 6 5 4 3 2 1

One Special Summer

POLLY'S STORY

Chapter One

"Hello, Polly?" said the voice on the phone. "It's Susan."

Holding the phone with my shoulder, I stood on one foot and slipped my other foot into my shoe. It was typical that I had to dash out of the shower, throw a bathrobe around me, and bolt for the phone from the other end of the house while my brother, Pearce, sat watching television not ten feet away. Pearce doesn't answer phones.

"Hi, Susan," I said. "Hang on." I reached for a kitchen towel and wrapped it around my head to stop the steady drip from my hair to the carpet.

"Just called to say hello," Susan continued. "Have you done the algebra yet?"

"Yep."

"Lucky you," groaned Susan. Pause. "Is Pearce there?"

1

"Sure," I said. "Want to talk to him?"

Susan squealed, "Noooo! Just wondered. You know." She giggled. "What's he wearing?"

I looked over at Pearce settled down with a bowl of potato chips in front of some quiz show. It didn't seem worth going into what he was wearing—worn-out cut-offs split up the side so far his underwear was showing. The only sign of life he showed was wiggling his bare toes.

"I don't know," I said. From the way my friends hung on to Pearce's every move, you would have thought he was a rock star. What always surprised me was that none of them seemed to notice that behind that gorgeous profile was an ordinary guy who left his dirty socks in the hall. I changed the subject back to school. "The algebra isn't that hard, Susan. I did it in study hall, and it only took half an hour. It's the same stuff Mrs. Stiles covered in class."

"Maybe it only took *you* half an hour. It'll take me forever," she said. "Is Pearce going out tonight?"

"I don't know," I said. "Look, Susan, I'm standing here dripping. I'd better go," I said.

When I hung up, Pearce looked at me and grinned. I guessed he had heard that Susan was asking about him and thought it was funny. "You *could* answer the phone once in a while," I said.

"It's always for you, anyway," he said, crunching into another potato chip.

Mom opened the back door, scraped the dirt off her shoes, and came in. "Finished with the pansies, anyway," she said with satisfaction.

I put my case to her. "Mom, don't you think Pearce could answer the phone once in a while? I had to run all the way from the shower to get it, and he was right here and didn't budge.''

"Well, most of the calls are for you, dear," Mom said.

I knew when I was outnumbered. Besides, I had to admit there was some truth to what they were saying. Ever since I'd started high school and was in the same school with Pearce and his friends, I'd been getting an awful lot of phone calls from my friends. I would have liked to think my sudden popularity had to do with my great personality, but actually it was pretty clear that Pearce was the attraction, him and all those friends of his from the swimming team who hung out at our house. Suddenly, that year, everybody I knew couldn't wait to come over to get my help with algebra or biology. The idea was to get a ringside seat for the parade of boys that streamed through the house. If only they had realized that as far as Pearce's friends were concerned, freshman girls did not exist.

The doorbell rang. Pearce's friends, of course. They never called, just showed up at our doorstep holding a basketball or football, depending on the season. I made a getaway so I could get dressed in something a little more attractive than a wet bathrobe and towel. Not that anyone would notice.

In my bedroom, I got into my jeans and a shirt and began blowing my hair dry. The warm swoosh of air and the hypnotic roar of the dryer almost put me to sleep. In a loud mechanical hum, the blow dryer seemed to talk:

> *Zeeeeeeeeeee,Zeeeeeeeeee,*
> *Polly is my cup of tea.*
> *Whuuuuuuurl, Whuuuuuuurl,*
> *Polly is a pretty girl.*

3

If I got as much positive feedback from everybody as I got from my hair dryer, my life would be perfect.

Once the dryer was off, I could hear the *pock-pock* of the basketball on the driveway outside. I parted the blinds and peeked out. There must have been six or seven boys out there. Pearce's friends run in packs.

Mother poked her head in my door. "Polly, would you take a tray of cookies and drinks out to the boys? I want to divide those day lilies before supper."

It was Mom's policy to keep the cookies and refreshments coming whenever anyone came over. That was her way of encouraging Pearce's friends to hang out at our house instead of the video arcade, and it was almost one hundred percent effective. I headed for the kitchen to get things ready for the hungry herd. As I passed through the family room on my way to the kitchen, I switched off the television Pearce had left on and picked up the empty potato chip bowl. Sometimes it seemed to me there wasn't much difference between being a kid sister and being a maid.

I made a big pile of chocolate chip cookies on the plate, filled a huge pitcher with Gatorade, and headed out toward the basketball hoop. What I really needed for transporting the pounds of food Pearce and his friends ate was a wheelbarrow. Maybe I would try one sometime.

"Chow time," I called. The game stopped in midplay, and all the guys charged toward the picnic table. No one looked at me. I might as well have still had the dishtowel on my head for all the attention I got. Adam Renfrow did say, "Thanks, Molly." "Polly. It's Polly," I murmured hopelessly.

I went back in the house. Mother was peeling off her gardening gloves. "Have you thought about the swim tryouts for next year, Polly?" she asked.

4

Mom and Dad were trying to get me to follow in Pearce's footsteps, or I should say wake. He started out swimming freshman year on our high school's championship team. I was a good swimmer, too, but I didn't want to spend my whole life following after Pearce. What I needed was to get away from Pearce—completely away.

"A person needs to have a sport," said Mother. "It gives you a sense of proportion." Heading toward the kitchen, she added, "I think of gardening as my sport."

I grinned. If being buried in seed catalogs from December to March, poking around in a compost heap from March to June, and worrying about insect damage from June to September was having a sense of proportion, then Mom had a terrific one.

A little while later I looked out the back window. All of the boys had left except Mac Chambless, Pearce's best friend. He and Pearce were sitting in the lawn chairs in the backyard, bent over a book. Strictly speaking, Mac wasn't the best-looking of Pearce's friends, but he was the nicest. He had been hanging around our house as long as I could remember and was my first choice as to who I'd like to be lost on a desert island with—broad-shouldered, with big hands, and a kind of rumpled look, as if he had always just come in from a windstorm. I stood at the window looking at him for a good five minutes. I seemed to be spending a lot of time looking out windows at boys. That was my life—look, but don't touch. A parade of boys went through our house every week, but for all they noticed me, they might as well have been on a movie screen.

Mother came out of the kitchen. "Polly, why don't you ask Mac if he'd like to stay for supper," she said. "Then maybe you can fix the carrots. The pot roast is almost done."

The garden was thick with spring smells as I made my way back to the lawn chairs. Even the dirt where Mother had been digging pansies smelled good.

"Mom wants to know if you'd like to stay for dinner, Mac," I said. "There's plenty of pot roast."

"Come on and stay," Pearce urged him.

"I'll have to give Mom a call," said Mac. "Hey, Polly, how's that research paper coming?"

That was one of the nice things about Mac. He remembered what was going on in my life. "It's finished," I said happily. "Would you like to read it?" Mac is really interested in history, and he had lent me some books for my paper on Franklin Roosevelt.

"Mac doesn't want to read your dumb research paper," said Pearce, rudely.

I felt sorry for any girl who married Pearce. Nobody would ever say he had an even disposition. I ignored his last remark and craftily pointed out that the mail had come. He disappeared in a streak, hoping for a letter from his girlfriend, Leila. I was pleased at myself for managing to have a few minutes alone with Mac. Being with him was like warming your hands at a fire. "Mr. Dixon loved the paper," I said. "The books you lent me were a big help." Mac was listening attentively with his head cocked a bit to one side in that way he has. I was encouraged enough to try to make an intelligent remark. "I thought it was really interesting reading about Roosevelt's advisors and all the things they did," I said.

"Yeah," said Mac thoughtfully. "I've always been interested myself in what really went on behind the scenes during important times in history."

I might have tried to keep up the conversation, but when Pearce reappeared with that glowing face that meant Leila had come through with a letter, I remembered I had to get to the carrots and faded back into the house.

From my point of view, Mac was just about perfect. But even apart from the fact that he obviously had me pegged in the role of baby sister, I had been discouraged lately to realize that I was not his type. One thing I had learned from having a brother was that different boys liked different types of girls. For instance, maybe because Pearce was blond and moody, all his girlfriends had dark hair and a kind of simpering sweetness. It almost never failed. What was discouraging about Mac was that I had seen him out with Nancy Jane Patterson, and there was no denying that she and I were completely different. I'm a blond like Nancy Jane, but she has the kind of long, sleek, almost platinum hair that seems to whisper the names of exotic things, while I have the kind of soft, short blond hair that reminds you of baby chicks. If I wore that dark lipstick she wears, I would just end up looking embalmed, and since I actually use my fingers, it wouldn't be practical for me to have nails as long as hers, either. The fact is, Nancy Jane is a sophisticated type while I am more a fresh-air type. There was nothing that could be done about it. Mac would just have to go on being a big brother to me.

Back in the kitchen, I set about scraping carrots, making nice, neat curls into the sink.

Curl, curl, Polly is a gorgeous girl . . .

A girl has to get her compliments where she can. Next I'd be sending myself flowers.

Dad was working late and wasn't home for supper, so we were glad to have Mac's help eating the pot roast. If we ate it all up at one meal, we were saved from Mom's experiments in exciting leftovers. Pearce and I had some grim memories

7

of Pot Roast Supreme, Pot Roast Surprise, and a recipe we called Pot Roast Sinister.

At the dinner table, Pearce was all sunshine. "Good pot roast," he said, taking a second helping. "Say, Polly, how'd you like me to help you build those bookshelves of yours?"

I didn't know what Leila had said in her letter, but I wished I could bottle it. I had books all over the floor of my bedroom and hadn't gotten much further with the bookshelves than buying a ton of plywood and a little paperback called *Build Your Own Bookshelves*. One night I had gone so far as to take out Dad's electric hand-saw, but I needed a helping hand to get motivated to actually do the job.

"Gee, that would be great," I breathed. "I really would appreciate it, Pearce. Could we get started on it tomorrow night?" I was anxious to get moving on it before the bloom wore off his good mood.

"Can't tomorrow," he said. "How about Thursday?"

I would have liked to get him to sign an oath in blood, but since we had a guest for dinner, I controlled myself and just said, "Great."

Mom smiled. She loved it when Pearce and I were getting along. "Birdies in the nest agree," she used to say to us when we were little and life was constant warfare. After a few years, Pearce finally got old enough to notice that in real life, when birdies are in the nest, it's every bird for himself, and he pointed out to Mom that he and I *did* get along like birds in a nest—awful. Things had gotten more peaceful between us once we got older. Our relationship had improved a lot since the days when he used to run off with my security blanket and threaten to drop my teddy bear in the bathtub. Now he was less out to make me cry and more out to protect me, as if I were a three-year-old idiot. I didn't really hold that against him. I didn't even hold it against him that all my friends had crushes on him and that my life was completely overshadowed by him. It wasn't his fault. But I didn't want to go on living this way. It was driving me crazy.

That night, after dinner, Penelope came over to get my biology notes for the days she'd been out with a cold. Penelope has been my best friend since seventh grade. I don't think I have to say any more about her than this—no one ever calls her Penny. She's got what my mother calls strength of character.

"Where's Pearce?" she asked, looking around.

"He's gone," I said. "You know, I'm getting tired of people asking about Pearce. Susan calls to get a complete report on what he's wearing and what he's doing, and now you. I thought you came over to see me, not Pearce."

"Don't be ridiculous, Polly," she said. "I know Pearce too well to be mooning after him." She put her biology book on the table and smiled. "But I do like to keep an eye on those guys that follow him around."

I threw up my hands.

"You don't know how lucky you are," Penelope went on, "to have this smorgasbord of boys served up to you every day. You can look them over and take your pick."

"I'm not the draft board, you know," I said. "I can look them over all I want, but none of them even notices me."

"That's because they think of you as Pearce's little sister," Penelope said, looking pleased with herself as if she had said something terribly clever.

"Now look, Penelope. Having Pearce's gang hang out around here isn't as great as you think. All I get out of it is getting to help feed and clean up after them. And on top of it

9

all, I have to put up with feeling like my friends come over here just to see them. I feel like I'm being used.''

To give her credit, Penelope did look a little bit guilty. ''I did come over to see you, Polly. The boys are just a fringe benefit,'' she said. She settled down at the table and picked up my stack of notes. ''Don't think of it as people using you,'' she said. ''Just think of Pearce as one of the added attractions of your house, like your mother's cookies or your own sweet personality.''

It was no use. It was hopeless to think she was going to see it my way.

That night I dreamed I was flying on a magic carpet. That was one dream I didn't have to look up in the *Pocket Guide to Dreams*. Even I could see it was a dream about escape. I had that kind of dream a lot. I loved my family and friends, but they would have been surprised to know how much I wanted to get away from them. I wanted to live life on my own. I wanted to set off and see the world. But most of all, I wanted to get away from being Pearce's little sister.

Chapter Two

I have been a part of Mrs. MacDougal's stable of baby-sitters for a couple of years. I say "stable," because ever since the twins arrived, Mrs. M. has had to go in for baby-sitters in a bigger way than most people. Not only does she need to get out of the house more than the average mother in order to keep from going bonkers, but also sometimes she needs to hire two sitters at a time. Like if I'm going to have to feed the kids supper, she asks me to get a friend to come along, because it can be quite a handful.

Some sitters actually charge Mrs. MacDougal extra because she has three kids, but I like baby-sitting for her, partly because she's awfully nice and partly because the kids are a challenge. When the girls at school get together and tell horror stories about the MacDougal kids—like the time Brian locked himself in the bathroom, got his hand stuck in the toilet, and the baby-sitter had to call the fire department—it sort of perks me up to think I've never gotten in that kind of fix over there. You have to be alert at the MacDougals'. There's no sense kidding yourself that you can catch up on your homework there, but if you pay attention, I tell people, it is definitely possible to keep the kids from setting your hair on fire.

I guess I just like to baby-sit, period. Probably if you looked into it, it would turn out that the reason I like it is that it's so different from being a little sister: I get to be the *big* one for a change. There's another reason I like it, though, one that I don't tell just anybody. Baby-sitting is a part of my grand plan to be a nanny for a few years before I go to college. I guess that's an unusual ambition, and I don't plan to do it my whole life, but I do want to do it long enough to see the world. I want to live in Italy or France, one of those countries where people have nannies. I can see myself pushing a carriage along in a quaint park, riding a bicycle on cobbled streets. Of course, I would learn to speak the language fluently. Now, for nannying, I not only need foreign languages, but also child-care experience. That's where the baby-sitting comes in. I secretly think of baby-sitting as my ticket out of Fairview. I didn't expect it to be a ticket out, however, quite as soon as it turned out to be.

One afternoon I baby-sat for Mrs. MacDougal while she played tennis. Unless there's actually snow on the ground, Mrs. M. is out there batting the ball around once a week. Maybe that's why she doesn't look a bit like a woman who's being driven crazy by three small children. She's in her thirties, but she doesn't look all that different from girls in college. She's a small, dark-haired woman, and she looks very nice, I think, in a tennis dress. When she came in, instead of handing me my money right away and dashing to the shower the way she usually did, she sat down at the kitchen table and asked me, "Have you thought about getting a summer job this year, Polly?" I hadn't really, because the competition is so stiff among the kids who are sixteen that it's a waste of time for anybody younger to try for a job. "We're going to Silver Beach for the summer," she went on, coming right to the point, "and I wonder if you would like to go with us and work as a mother's helper."

At first I didn't know what to say. It came over me that I wanted to go so bad I could hardly stand it. Here was my chance to get away from this whole business of being Pearce's sister. And to Silver Beach!

"I'll have to ask my parents," I said, when I got my breath.

"Of course," said Mrs. MacDougal. "I'll talk it over with them myself. But I thought I would check with you first to see if you were interested."

Interested? I was so interested I couldn't see straight. Nobody was home yet when I got back to the house, and I was bursting with my news, so I called Penelope.

"Silver Beach?" she squealed. "You'll love it! You'll absolutely love it! The place is wall-to-wall gorgeous guys with tans."

"I'm not sure Mom and Dad will let me go," I said uncertainly.

"Oh, sure they will. They know Mrs. MacDougal will keep an eye on you."

As it turned out, Penelope was right. Mom had a long talk with Mrs. MacDougal. Then she and Dad said I could go. It was so easy I couldn't quite believe it. At one point I almost wondered if Mom and Dad were keen to get rid of me. Another time I started thinking that maybe I would hate it and have a terrible time. But most of the time I was just counting the days until summer vacation would begin.

"It's quite a compliment," Mom said, "that Mrs. MacDougal has chosen you out of all the baby-sitters who work for her."

"I know," I said. Actually, for all I knew, the other sitters had demanded combat pay or turned her down flat, but I didn't go into that with Mom.

"It's not going to be like living at home," Mom warned. "You're going to be more on your own."

That didn't discourage me a bit. It was just what I was hoping for.

The rest of the spring, until school was out, just knowing that I was going to get away made me easier to get along with. No matter how much something might get to me, I knew I was only going to have to put up with it for a while longer. One day Margie Jackson walked up to me in the hall and sighed, "Gee, it must be great to be Pearce's sister." In the old days I would have had to work hard to overcome the desire to hit her on the head with my notebook, but then— with the summer so close—I was able to smile. What did I care? In June I would be on my way to Silver Beach.

Finally the magic day came. I was waiting with my suitcases and duffel bag when the MacDougals came by to pick me up. I climbed into the backseat of the van with the twins. Behind us in the van were the high chairs, the playpen, and more stuff crammed in than you would have thought a family would need for a lifetime, let alone a summer at the beach.

"It's a little crowded," said Mr. MacDougal, heaving one

14

of my suitcases in between a tower of boxes of disposable diapers and a stack of linens. "Maybe you'd better put that duffel bag on the floor of the back seat."

Tracy took her sticky pacifier out of her mouth and, dimpling, offered it to me when I slid in beside her. Little did I know it, but this warm little moment was to be the high point of the whole trip.

It turned out that the kids cried most of the way there. I could see that I had been on the right track when I had decided to see the world before I had children of my own. Kids didn't exactly spur your sense of adventure. After hours in the car with the MacDougal kids, I felt so worn out I wouldn't have crossed the street to see the Taj Mahal. Riding with them, you got to where all you cared about was whether the upcoming Howard Johnson's had a changing table in the bathroom.

It was amazing, but in all the time I had been looking forward to going to Silver Beach, it hadn't really hit me until the day we drove over that Mrs. MacDougal had hired me to come along because she needed help, and she needed it bad. I had been so excited about getting away from home and from Pearce that I hadn't really thought about how the summer was going to be a very long baby-sitting job. When I came to think about it, I wasn't sure how much time I was going to have for the tanned boys and the beach parties Penelope had talked about. I hadn't even discussed the question of free time with Mrs. MacDougal.

After what seemed like a lifetime, Mr. MacDougal said, "Here we are!"

"At last," sighed Mrs. MacDougal faintly.

We had pulled up in the driveway of a cedar-shingled beach house, one of a row of houses that were on a street

15

within sight of the beach. There was some struggling grass in the sandy yard, some pines, and a few bushes. In the distance, sun sparkled on the water, and over us stretched the wide, empty sky. As I hoisted Tracy out of her safety seat, I realized that I didn't know a soul in Silver Beach. And I wasn't too sure how I would get to know anybody. I had lived my whole life in Fairview, and I hadn't had much practice getting to know new people. How did you go about it? Where did you find them? My heart sank. *Oh, dear, Polly,* I thought. *So far you're not making a very good world traveler.* If it was this bad being a mother's helper in Silver Beach, how would I feel being a nanny in Italy?

"Why don't we have Polly take the kids for a walk," said Mr. MacDougal, "while you and I unload."

"That's a good idea," said Mrs. MacDougal. She unloaded the big double stroller that both twins can ride in at once. It's so big you can't take it in stores, but it's just the thing for taking the kids for walks.

"Rruddun, ruddun, rruddun!" said Brian, making the sound of a revving engine. Brian is a compact five-year-old with red hair and a look of mischief that makes him stand out in any crowd. He is fascinated by machinery, and if he could be anything he wanted when he grew up, he would probably be a cement truck. *"Rruddun, ruddun!* Come on, Polly," he said.

Mr. and Mrs. MacDougal were already staggering toward the house like ants, carrying loads that looked bigger than they were. I lifted the twins into the stroller, and we set off on our walk. We didn't make fast progress, though. There was a fire hydrant right in front of the MacDougals' house, and we had to wheel over there so the twins could rattle its chains. Then Brian found a box turtle and had to be persuaded that it really did not want to come and live with him for the summer. By the time we finished that and were about to move along down the sidewalk, a girl about my age and a little boy came out of the house next door. Brian ran around in a big circle, kicking up sand and yelling, *"Ruddun, ruddun!"* Then he skidded to a stop in front of them and shouted, "My name's Brian. What's yours?"

I lifted the front wheels of the stroller up and managed to move it over the clumps of grass in the yard and toward the girl and her little brother.

"We're just moving in next door," I said, "for the summer. I'm Polly Barron." The girl smiled at me. She was a curvy blond with a perfect tan. In fact, she looked just the way I would have liked to look myself. I guessed she was a year or two older than me. "Lindsay Ellis," she said. "And this is my brother, Ben." She glanced at the twins, who were already cross at having nothing to do and were beginning to amuse themselves by pulling each other's hair. "You have three?" said Lindsay. "And I thought I was bad off with one kid brother."

"Oh, I'm just baby-sitting," I explained quickly. "I'll be helping Mrs. MacDougal out this summer."

Brian and Lindsay's brother were now running around in circles together, whooping like Indians. "I was just going to take Ben to the park to play," said Lindsay. "Do you all want to come with us?" She added, "It has a fence around it."

That sounded good to me. I called to Mrs. MacDougal that we were going to walk to the park with Lindsay. "O.K." she smiled, backing into the front door carrying a goosenecked reading lamp and a broom.

The park turned out to be only a couple of blocks away, toward the southern tip of the island. It was nothing fancy—a couple of swings, a sliding board, and some climbing toys—but it did have the wonderful fence Lindsay had mentioned and even a little gate so you didn't have to keep going through that business of counting the kids every few seconds. With a fence, the kids might still fall on their heads, but at least they weren't going to suddenly disappear if you stooped to tie your shoelace.

"Do you live here all year?" I asked Lindsay.

"No," she said. "We're from Chapel Hill. But we've come over every summer now for years. My father teaches at UNC, so he usually has the whole summer off. He's a biologist, so we come over here, and he counts barnacles and stuff and writes papers on it."

So Lindsay was a professor's daughter. She didn't look like a professor's daughter. I don't know what I expected one to look like, but Lindsay wasn't it. She slipped out of her sandals and stretched out a bare tanned foot.

"You certainly have a beautiful tan!" I said.

Lindsay smiled complacently. "It's just getting started," she said. "I work on it. I start before we even get here. I lie in the backyard catching rays while other people are still picking daffodils. That way I get a little bit of a head start. In another month it ought to be *really* good."

"I couldn't get a tan like that," I said sadly, "if I worked on it my whole life."

Lindsay glanced at my pale skin and cast about for some words of consolation. "Well, it's not as if a tan is the only thing that counts," she said. "You look very nice just the way you are."

I stifled a sigh. I didn't want to look "very nice." I wanted to look like Lindsay. But I appreciated her effort to cheer me

18

up. "Is it very hard to get to know people around here?" I asked.

"Oh, no. Everybody's very friendly. You get to know people pretty fast. Tell you what. Why don't you come with me to Miranda's party this weekend and I'll introduce you to some people."

"But I haven't been invited," I said.

"Silver Beach isn't like that," said Lindsay. "Everybody goes to the parties. On a small island like this, you can't go picking and choosing. You'd hurt people's feelings. Of course, I'll tell Miranda I'm bringing you along."

"That's nice of you," I said. "But I'm not sure whether Mrs. MacDougal is going to need me or not."

"Just explain to her about the party," said Lindsay. "Probably she'll be giving you Saturday nights off, anyway."

"We haven't talked about time off yet," I admitted.

"Well, of course you'll have some time off," said Lindsay. "All the girls who work as mother's helpers do. It's all scheduled around the big events of the island, of course. Nobody wants to give you Monday off because that's the day the club is closed and there isn't much for the kids to do on that day. And nobody will give you Wednesday off because this summer that's when the bridge club is meeting. But you've got to have some kind of time off."

"I guess so," I said meekly.

The twins were sitting on the ground sifting sand through their fingers, while Lindsay's brother and Brian were climbing around on the jungle gym with the coordination of orangutans. Brian is a pretty athletic five-year-old, but he had met his match in Ben, who acted like he had suction cups on his knees.

19

"Ben is pretty good on the jungle gym, isn't he?" I commented.

Lindsay regarded him without enthusiasm. "I guess so," she said. "Daddy thinks that he's got himself an all-American this time." She added, "I got demoted the minute Ben was born. It's a lucky thing it happened after my formative years, or I would probably be a warped personality. I didn't know it until Ben was born, but Daddy wanted a boy all along. You wouldn't believe all the footballs and electric trains around our house." Lindsay slipped her sandals back on. "Do you have a brother?" she asked.

I jumped guiltily. "Uh, yes. But I don't think my father favors him, exactly."

I could tell Lindsay was a nice person because she just looked happy for me. "That's great," she said warmly. "What's he like, your brother?"

"Uh, just an ordinary brother," I said weakly. I didn't want to get started on Pearce. I'd start sounding like the warped personality Lindsay had been talking about.

"Your parents have the right idea," said Lindsay. "Now with Ben, I have to keep reminding myself that it's not the poor little crumb's fault that Daddy's gaga about him. I shouldn't have to do that. When I have kids, I'm going to treat them exactly alike. That way there'll never be any trouble between them, and they'll all be good friends."

I gave a passing thought to the lack of perfect friendship between Pearce and me, but decided this was not the time to destroy Lindsay's illusions.

That night, I told Mrs. MacDougal about Miranda's party. "Of course you must go," she said. "Miranda's a very nice girl. I went to school with her mother. I always think Miranda has such a pretty face."

From this I got the idea Miranda was overweight, because that's what my mother always says when a girl could stand to lose twenty pounds.

"We'll have to work out a regular time off for you," Mrs. MacDougal went on, "as soon as I find out when the bridge club is meeting this year."

Chapter Three

Mr. MacDougal caught a ride back to Fairview the next day with a neighbor, leaving the van for Mrs. MacDougal to use. I thought he looked pretty cheerful and carefree as he left. I wondered if he was looking forward to a week without getting orange juice spilled in his lap.

Mrs. M. and I had our hands full. In spite of all the things that had been stuffed in the van, there were still a lot of things we came up missing. Mrs. M. started making lists. It turned out she was a great maker of lists. "Now, these are things Jack can bring over with him when he comes this weekend," she said. "And these are the things I had better go out and get." I kept the kids while she went out in the van to get groceries and things that just couldn't wait, like Band-Aids. We used an awful lot of Band-Aids.

Later, Mrs. MacDougal and I tried to take the kids to the beach, but it turned out the twins were just terrified of the waves. "Oh, dear," said Mrs. MacDougal. "I hoped they would have outgrown that by now. Well, tomorrow we'll take them to the club pool." She brightened. "They have a fence around the whole thing."

The Silver Beach Country Club pool was a nice place and pretty close to us, too, but we had to pile a good bit of stuff into the van before we set off—water wings, towels, suntan lotion, beach robes, playpen, and (of course) Band-Aids. I don't see how Mrs. MacDougal could ever have gotten that stuff unloaded if I hadn't been there. Somebody had to keep the kids corralled while she was getting the playpen out of the back of the van. If I hadn't been there, Brian and the twins would have run and jumped off the high dive by the time she had gotten everything unloaded. Once we had carried everything over to the pool, I took Brian into the big pool and Mrs. M. took the twins over to the shallow baby pool. The air was hot, but since it was early in the summer, the water was still cold. Brian jumped right in. "It's n-not cold," he said, his skin turning blue. "It's just right." He bobbed under and came up spouting water.

I knew the thing to do was just to plunge right in and get it over with, so I gritted my teeth and slid in. "It's not cold, is it?" said Brian, laughing.

There was a splash near us as a kid came down the water slide. Brian's eyes began to glitter. "I want to go down the slide, O.K., Polly? I'm going to go down the slide."

I was glad to be the one in the water waiting at the foot of the slide to catch him instead of being poor Brian, shivering in the breeze while he stood in line waiting for his turn at the

24

slide. But he was loving it. Kids have their own idea of a good time.

"Polly!" someone called.

I looked around and saw Lindsay with Ben in tow. I waved. Ben dived into the water with a big splash. "It's not cold, Lindsay!" he shrieked. "It's just right."

"Thanks," said Lindsay wryly, "I'll watch."

Brian came down the slide with a swoosh, and I caught him in my arms. "Look, Ben is here!" I told him.

"Watch me be a shark!" Ben yelled at us. He dived under water, keeping one hand out to represent a fin, then came up sputtering. "Did you see my fin, Polly?" he said.

"I can swim faster than you," Brian challenged him.

Soon Brian and Ben were flailing around trying to beat each other swimming the width of the shallow end. I paddled over to where Lindsay was sitting on the edge of the pool.

"Are you going to be able to make it to the party?" she asked. "I told Miranda I'd probably be bringing you."

"I think I can come," I said. "Mrs. MacDougal said I could."

"I won!" shouted Brian at my side. "I can swim the fastest."

Ben howled, "You did not! I won! I won! Didn't I win, Lindsay?"

"It looked like a tie to me," said Lindsay. "You both won."

"Let's do it again," said Ben, plunging under again.

"This is how I earn my allowance, keeping Ben," Lindsay sighed. "Sometimes I ask myself if it's worth it."

Over at the far end of the pool, I could see eight or ten kids our age gathered in a circle. They seemed to be playing some sort of game in the water. One of the boys lifted up a girl with long black hair and carried her sitting on his shoulders. She waved at us.

"That's Mona," Lindsey explained to me, waving back. "You'll meet her at the party. In fact, you'll see them all at the party."

From this distance they all looked sleek as porpoises and very good-looking. I couldn't think what I'd say to them if I did meet them.

Now that I had seen the circle of kids, I was filled with worry about Miranda's party. "What will people be wearing to the party?" I asked.

"Oh, jeans, swimsuits, dresses—any old thing."

That didn't give me much to go on.

By the time Saturday night rolled around, I felt as if I deserved a little recreation. My only fear was that the party wasn't going to be it. I had settled on wearing jeans, figuring that everywhere you went somebody, at least, would be wearing jeans. But when Lindsay stopped by to pick me up, she was wearing a beautiful low-cut cotton sundress and big gold hoop earrings. I wanted to go change, but she pulled me out the door. "Don't be silly," she said. "You look fine."

When we drove up to Miranda's house, we could hear the music before we got out of the car. "She has a live band," purred Lindsay contentedly. "Nice." As we slid out of the car, Lindsay said, "I love to dance."

We went around to where the crowd was gathered on the deck at the back of the house. I could see the band standing on a small platform near the deck. *Crash!* went the drums. Miranda came forward to meet us. I recognized her right away by her being twenty pounds overweight. I was relieved to see that she was wearing jeans. "I'm glad you could come,

26

Polly," she said. I was very impressed that she remembered my name. I wasn't able to find out any more about her, because there was such a crush of kids I didn't see her again the whole evening.

"This is Art," Lindsay said enthusiastically, introducing me to a tall, thin boy with pale eyelashes, "the best dancer in Silver Beach."

As soon as Art and Lindsay found a clear spot on the deck, they started dancing. I was without my chief introducer, so I got a soft drink and sat down on the bench that ran along the edge of the deck. A boy in a kelly green-and-yellow striped polo shirt sat down next to me and watched Art and Lindsay dance. Other couples were dancing, but they were nowhere as good as Art and Lindsay.

"Do you like to dance?" he asked me.

I wasn't sure if this was an invitation or not. "I guess I like it O.K.," I said cautiously.

"I hate it, too," he said. "My name's Allen Winkle. What's yours?"

"Polly Barron."

"Barron," he said musingly. "Barron. Seems like one time I swam against a guy named Barron in a district meet."

"Oh?" I said politely. "Are you going to be here all summer?" I asked hastily. I wanted to change the subject quick before we started exploring the question of what relative of mine could have been at that swim meet. I hadn't gone to all that trouble to get away from Pearce in order to sit around discussing his backstroke.

"Yep. I'll be here all summer. I have a job at the snack bar at the country club."

"I have a job, too," I said. "I'm a mother's helper."

He grinned. "I'd rather dish up hamburgers," he said.

It's funny how many people don't like to take care of kids. Children are people, and a lot more interesting than hamburgers.

"Want to dance?" said Allen.

"O.K.," I said. I wasn't sure what to expect after hearing how Allen hated to dance, but he was an all right dancer, like a person who had taken lessons once when he was a kid.

"When there's dancing," he said, "I always grab the first slow dance, then when it gets fast and complicated I drop out and eat a hot dog."

The colored lights strung up all around the deck made everybody look a little unreal, splashing their faces with red and green as they danced by, but now that I got a close look at Allen I could see he wasn't at all an unattractive guy. He had nice brown eyes and looked as if he was used to seeing the funny side of things.

As he had promised, when the band heated up he led me over to the hot dogs. Quite a few kids were already clustered there by the steam tray for the hot dogs and the big tubs of ice studded with cans of soft drinks. "Polly," Allen said, "meet Skip Harris." Skip was a completely different type from Allen. He had close-cropped blond hair, which lay thick against his head like a lion's pelt, and startling blue eyes. He was built like a football tackle except that he was on the small side, and he was wearing an old sweatshirt with the sleeves hacked off.

The girl with hip-length black hair next to him smiled and said, "I'm Mona."

"Oh, yes. Forgot Mona," said Allen, hitting his head with his hand. I didn't see how anybody could forget Mona. She was positively magnetic with that swinging, long black hair. I realized that they were some of the kids I had seen at the pool earlier in the week. Up close, they looked friendly.

"Miranda always throws the first party of the year," said Mona enthusiastically. "And they're always terrific."

"They're O.K., if you like to dance," said Skip.

"Skip would rather play volleyball," said Mona.

"So what?" said Skip. "Volleyball is more fun."

Allen's soft drink can made a soft popping sound as he opened it. "That's all right, Skip," he said. "When you and I have a party, we won't have dancing."

Mona looked uncomfortable. "What if Miranda should hear you?" she said.

Skip looked at Mona coolly. "You know, Mona," he said, "if you cut that hair you would have better peripheral vision."

Mona's eyes flashed fire.

"I think your hair is just gorgeous," I said quickly. "I would never cut it." It did occur to me, though, after Skip said that, that Mona's hair must be impractical in some ways. I wondered if it felt heavy and whether it took long to dry once it got wet. When she sat down, did she have to sweep it out from under her to keep from sitting on it? Did she ever get it caught in doors as she closed them behind her? But it did look great. I decided right then to let my hair grow out the rest of the summer.

"Better watch your step, Skip," said Allen, "or Mona might strangle you with that hair."

Mona laughed. I got the idea that she kind of liked Allen and there wasn't much he could say that would get to her.

In a minute Lindsay and her dancing partner joined us, breathless from dancing. I noticed that Lindsay's blond hair took on a green tint from the colored light, and I wondered if I looked that way, too. I didn't want to make my first impression looking like a St. Patrick's Day leprechaun. I stole a glance at the lights and edged over closer to a pink one. I could remember being told that pink is flattering.

"I see you found the gang," Lindsay panted, fishing around in the ice for a soft drink. "Have they been telling you all sorts of lies?"

Allen put his arm around her. "Ah, Lindsay, my life, my love. You know I could never tell a lie."

Lindsay pecked him on the cheek. "Of course not, dear," she said easily.

I couldn't figure out if there was a romance blossoming between Allen and Lindsay or not. On the whole, I decided not. Especially when I remembered how Allen hated to dance. The thought drifted through my mind that they were putting on a bit of a show for me because I was someone new. They were interested in me. It was a strange and nice feeling to think that people were looking at me as an interesting possibility and wondering what I was like. So often at home I had felt like I was permanently in the background compared to Pearce. It was nice to have the spotlight on me for a change.

I looked around me at all the kids moving around in the colored lights and realized that I was really enjoying myself. It was so different from the way things were in Fairview, where I had known everybody as long as I could remember.

Later on I danced with Art Fulford, the boy with the pale eyelashes and "the best dancer in Silver Beach." I found out that he would be a senior next year, the same age as Pearce. Lindsay, Mona, and Allen were all going to be juniors, but Skip was a year younger, my age. Age didn't seem to be as important here at Silver Beach as it had been at home. Everybody just hung around with whoever they liked. Maybe that was because we weren't in school, and whether someone was old enough to drive didn't matter much, either, because you could get around the whole beach pretty well without driving.

"What do you like to do, Polly?" Art asked me, peering at me seriously through his pale eyelashes.

I realized that I had never before had so many guys looking straight at me as if they realized I was a girl. I liked it, but it ruined my concentration. Also, Art was a really good dancer and I was trying hard to keep up to his standard, so it was hard to talk at the same time.

"I like to swim," I said. "And read." That might not go down as the most fascinating answer in history, but at least I got it out.

"Ah, unusual interests," he said.

I wondered if he were making fun of me but decided to give him the benefit of the doubt. "What do you like to do?" I said politely.

"I like to dance," he said, pulling off a tricky maneuver that nearly left me sitting on the drums.

I decided I probably wouldn't be seeing much of Art. He could tell by now that for first-class dancing he'd have to look somewhere else.

When we halted at the drink cooler, Lindsay found us. "Are you getting ready to go home, Polly?" she said. "I told Mrs. MacDougal we wouldn't be late getting in."

I was happy to hear it. I'm one of those people who is ready for a cup of hot milk and bed by eleven, but I didn't tell just anybody that—it sounded too disgustingly wholesome. "Maybe we *had* better be going," I said. "I wouldn't want to worry her."

Art took Lindsay's hand. "One more dance, lady," he said. Her eyes lit up. Those two really could dance. I leaned

31

over the rail of the deck and looked at the band. They were beginning to look pretty tired. I supposed they must have regular jobs during the week. Maybe they were plumbers or high school math teachers. I had never been to a party with a live band before, so I found them very interesting.

Lindsay appeared at my side. "Ready?" she said with a satisfied sigh. She turned to wave goodbye to Art as we walked down the stairs to the deck. The night was turning cool, and I was just as glad I hadn't worn a sundress.

As we drove home, I thought about whether I should ask Lindsay about some of the kids at the party. It would be interesting to know what she thought about everybody, but on the other hand, maybe it was better for me to wait and form my own opinion.

"Do you think you're going to like Silver Beach?" she said.

I leaned back against the seat. "Yes," I said happily. "I think I'm going to like it a lot."

It was beginning to feel like a wonderful summer.

Chapter Four

It was amazing how much I did like Silver Beach. Of course, there were some things that took some getting used to. Mom had been right; I was more on my own. I had more responsibilities at the MacDougals'. And sometimes I felt the strain of living with a family that had different ways of doing things. After all, I had lived with my own family my whole life and knew just what they expected of me, while with Mrs. MacDougal I had to feel my way.

One thing I found out about myself after those first few awkward days, though, was that it didn't bother me getting to know new people and new ways of doing things. It was kind of fun. Besides getting to know the MacDougals much better, I got to know all the kids in Lindsay's crowd. We went around together a lot.

I decided that Art, the good dancer, really liked Lindsay. You could watch his eyes follow her all over the room. But he was an odd sort of guy—quiet. Sometimes when I was out with the kids in the backyard at the crack of dawn, I'd see him walking by himself on the beach. You could tell it was him, even from a distance, because he was so slender and his hair was so pale. I think he knew that to Lindsay he was just a good dancer, nothing more.

Skip, in spite of those angelic blue eyes of his, didn't seem like a completely nice person to me. He was kind of likely to make cold, critical remarks, although most of the time you didn't notice it.

Mona turned out to be the most ordinary person of the bunch. With that long hair, she looked really dramatic, but she was the sort of person who talked about the decorations at a party as if that were a really interesting subject. She could get all excited telling you how she was going to get a Princess telephone for her birthday. She was awfully nice to me, so I felt guilty even thinking it, but the fact was she was a little bit boring.

Lindsay became my best friend. She was someone I could really talk to. And after years of having Penelope as my best friend, I found Lindsay sort of restful. Penelope's strength of character can sometimes wear a person down. Every now and then I realized that I didn't know what Lindsay thought about something, and that, I decided, was one of the nice things about her. She wasn't always telling you what she thought.

Next to Lindsay, Allen was my favorite. He could make me laugh. He took to hanging around me at the parties and at the pool. It wasn't a romance exactly, but it was a lot better than being ignored. At first I kept bracing myself for him to make a move. *What will I do*, I thought, *if he tries to kiss me? What will I say if he asks if he can come by and pick me up for a party?* But as the weeks went on, I realized that he probably wasn't going to do any of those things. He was just going to hang around. Still, I was pretty happy with that and with the way things were in general.

As the weeks went by I began to get a tan of sorts, though I had to take it very slowly. I'm not one of those people who can just paint themselves with baby oil and go out and bake. But after a while I began to look a little less like a marshmallow and a little more like a piece of toast. As my skin got darker my hair got lighter, and it wasn't very long before I quit wishing that I looked like Lindsay (which was hopeless anyway, as I will never have that much bosom) and was happy enough to look like myself.

What I realized finally was that all that time I used to spend looking out the window at Pearce's friends and wishing they'd suddenly whisper sweet nothings in my ear, what I probably wanted most of all was just for people to treat me like a regular person—a main course, not a side dish to Pearce. The proof of this was that no one had whispered sweet nothings in my ear since I got to Silver Beach, and yet I was perfectly happy. I just couldn't seem to get over the pleasure of never having people ask me about Pearce. It seemed too good to be true that none of these people had ever heard about what a great swimmer he was and how good-looking he was. Because I felt that way, running into Mac, Pearce's best friend, was a terrible shock. I was sure it was going to ruin my whole summer.

The day Mac showed up was a day like any other. The sun was shining itself silly, and Mrs. M. and I had the kids at the club pool. Brian's swimming was coming along nicely. I was sitting on the edge of the pool, dangling my legs in the warm

35

water and cheering him on, when suddenly I noticed that the lifeguard at the other end of the pool didn't look familiar. The lifeguard we'd had up till then was a skinny guy with brown hair. I'd never really gotten to know him, but he'd been at all the weekend parties, and of course he watched over us from his lifeguard chair every day at the pool. I peered at the new lifeguard, who was a big hulking guy, and realized suddenly that, far from looking *un*familiar, he looked *too* familiar. It was Mac! I reached quickly for my carryall and put on my sunglasses so that I could be incognito while I figured out what to do. Good grief! Mac!

A few weeks before, I had thought Mac was the guy I would most like to be stuck on a desert island with, but I didn't want him on that island—not right then. In fact, just looking at him over there made me feel two years younger. What was I going to do? Wear my sunglasses all summer? I had a moment of panic just thinking about it. Here I had been having such a wonderful time, and now who should show up but Pearce's best friend, ready to treat me like a three-year-old. Maybe he would even tell funny stories about when I was a little girl. Finally, though, a sane thought occurred to me. Mac had always been nice to me, but he'd never really paid that much attention to me, so why should he bother now? He'd find his own little group, latch onto some sophisticated-looking blond with long fingernails, and *poof!* —he would be out of my life as much as if he were still in Fairview.

Just as these sane thoughts began to win the day, Mac blew the whistle signaling break time, the ten minutes of each hour when lifeguards clear the pool and flake out. "Break!" "Break!" Mac and the other lifeguard, Brandon, were yelling.

Brian crawled up out of the pool unwillingly, his red hair

dripping. "Aw, I hate break," he said. I wrapped a towel around him. "Can we go get some french fries, huh, Polly?" he said.

"You know we can't go get french fries every time we have break," I said.

"Break is boring," he said.

"Would you like to go over to the baby pool for a little while with Tracy and Mark?" I asked.

"I hate the dumb old baby pool," he said crossly.

Just then Mac appeared practically at my elbow.

"Mac!" I said weakly. "So you're the new lifeguard." It was funny, but when Mac actually came up to me like that, for a minute I quit thinking about how I wished he had never shown up and thought it would be nice if he got even closer.

I introduced Brian, who gave Mac a good idea of his personality right off by whopping him one in the stomach. I quickly moved Brian out of hitting range. I knew from experience that you don't get far with him by threatening him or appealing to his conscience. Mac smiled at Brian. I realized that it must be easy to be tolerant if you're as big as Mac. Brian might be a terror in the sandbox set, but it was laughable to think he would make any dent in Mac.

"Polly," said Mac, "am I glad to see you! Tell me where everything is around here. I was called in as a replacement for the head guard, and no one's had time to show me the ropes."

I could see what he meant when he told me there weren't any signs anywhere. It *was* kind of confusing if you didn't have anybody to show you where things were. I tried to point out the main places necessary for survival, like the soft drink machine and the locker rooms. It was an odd sensation to be helping Mac out when at home he'd have been the one

37

helping me out. It was odd, too, to be there at Silver Beach where everything had been so different for me, and yet to have Mac beside me with his crooked smile, his down-to-earth face and mussed-up hair, looking just the same as always. When I thought of how nice he'd been to me my whole life, I felt guilty that when I first saw him I had wished he would disappear.

"I wanna get back in the pool," said Brian. "When is break going to be over, Polly?" I didn't feel like coping with Brian right then. I was too busy coping with my life. I tried to distract him by putting suntan lotion on him, while I sorted out my confusing feelings. Mac was stooping down next to me so close, I was finding it hard to think of anything else but him.

Just then Lindsay came up. "Hi, Polly," she said.

I looked up, shading my eyes from the sun that was beaming directly behind Lindsay. "Hi, Lindsay," I said. "This is Mac, a friend of my brother's from home."

Mac straightened up and smiled at her. I saw Lindsay's eyes widen as she took him in. "Hi, Mac," she said, in this spacey little voice I'd never heard her use before. I had the feeling that he was definitely Lindsay's type.

"Mac is taking over as the new head lifeguard," I explained.

Lindsay showed all the signs of falling apart at the seams. She tugged on a strand of her hair and licked her lips nervously. I hoped Mac didn't notice. I wouldn't want him to fall for Lindsay, but on the other hand, I didn't want him to think my friends were absolute idiots.

"Nice to meet you, Lindsay," said Mac.

"You'll have to bring Mac along to my party Saturday night," said Lindsay.

I hadn't known Lindsay was planning a party that Saturday, and I looked at her in amazement.

"Just a spur-of-the-moment beach party," she added hastily. I had the feeling the spur for the moment had been the sight of Mac. "I'm just now getting around to asking people."

"Sounds like fun," said Mac. "Thanks. Ooops. Look at the clock. Gotta go." He blew a shrill blast on his whistle. "Break's over!" he yelled. Little kids began plunging back into the pool. He gave us a grin and headed back to his station. It struck me that although Mac's job had a lot more glamor than mine, it was a kind of baby-sitting, too.

It wasn't until Mac was safely back in his lifeguard chair way over at the far end of the pool that Lindsay slid close to me and whispered, "What a gorgeous hunk of a guy."

Considering the shrieking all the little kids were doing all around us, I didn't think I had to whisper. "You think so?" I said calmly. "I wouldn't have thought you would call Mac good-looking."

Lindsay shivered. "Well, not good-looking, maybe," she said. "But there's something about him."

"Raw animal magnetism?" I suggested.

"Yes," she breathed. "I think that's it. Boy, I wish Ben brought home friends like that."

I started to explain to Lindsay that Mac looked upon me as a little sister, but I stopped myself. Why should I let Lindsay think there was an open season on Mac? Lindsay was my friend, and I wanted all the best for her. But I had to be realistic. It wasn't going to cheer me up any if Mac started giving Lindsay the romantic rush right under my nose. I cast a glance at her in her hot-pink swimsuit and her faultless deep tan (with a lot more tan showing than swimsuit) and stifled a sigh. I could feel it coming over me again, the yearning to look like Lindsay.

All that week Mac sat high in his lifeguard's chair while Brian and I swam under his watchful eye, so it wasn't as if I could ever forget he was there. And every now and then, he'd come over and say hello on his break. All I could think about was Mac, Mac, Mac. Sometimes I thought wistfully about how happy I had been before he came. Sometimes I thought how much I would like for him to fall in love with me. Sometimes I tried to persuade myself that if I were a person with real will power—like Penelope, for instance—I could just carry on my life as usual, as if he had never showed up. I was not very happy. It seemed like such a long time until Lindsay's beach party rolled around that Saturday.

Mac had said he would come by the MacDougals' to pick me up for the party; then I could show him where it was. Of course, anybody could tell where it was because the bonfire we always built on the beach could be seen for miles, but remembering how I had felt when I first got to the beach, I decided he probably wanted someone to introduce him to people, somebody familiar to be with until he got his bearings.

I spent an awfully long time deciding what to wear to the party. In fact, I spread out every single thing I had brought with me and tried on half of them. After all that, I decided on cut-offs and a sweatshirt. I picked the sweatshirt because when I'm in a sweatshirt you don't notice so much that I don't have a lot of bosom, and I picked the cut-offs because I have good legs. I wanted to dress very casually, as if I couldn't have cared less what Mac thought of me. It took me about an hour to do that, from the mascara on my lashes to the pale pink polish on my toes.

As I waited, I peered out the window toward the beach. It

40

wasn't dark yet but the bonfire was going, and kids were already gathering. I wondered if Mac had forgotten about the party and wasn't going to show up at all. How long should I wait before I went on without him? Just then the doorbell rang. Giving a quick goodbye to Mrs. MacDougal, I dashed out. Mac parked his bicycle at the house, and we walked down to the beach together. That walk down to the beach was probably the longest time I had ever been alone with Mac in my whole life. At least, it seemed like the longest time. I felt a lump in my throat. I was feeling sorry for myself, thinking of how long I had had a crush on Mac and about how he was ruining my beautiful summer. Just then he said, "Have you heard from Pearce?"

"No," I said. "He'll be leaving for Colorado in a couple of weeks, so I don't guess I'll be hearing from him for quite a while. Pearce isn't much of a letter writer."

"Except to Leila," said Mac.

"Oh, I guess he does write to Leila," I admitted.

As we got closer to the party, I started to feel better. Allen would be there. I could count on him to bring me cold drinks, tell me funny stories, and make me feel important. I would even be glad to see Mona. I wanted to surround myself with all the people I knew who made me feel like an interesting person. Then I could just pretend Mac wasn't even here. Partly from nervousness and partly because I was really looking forward to the party, I found myself babbling on about how I loved Silver Beach. I just longed to get away from Mac so I could feel like myself again. No sooner did we step foot on the beach than I ignored everything my mother had ever taught me about good manners and just faded into the crowd looking for Allen.

I found him sitting down, drawing in the sand, while Skip

and Mona looked on. "Give up?" he was saying. "It's a trombone player in a telephone booth." He looked up as I walked up. "Hi, Polly," he smiled. "We were wondering where you were."

"I was waiting for Mac, the new lifeguard," I said. "He's a friend of my brother's, and he came with me tonight."

"What happened to the old lifeguard?" said Skip.

"Some family emergency," I explained.

"Where is this guy, Mac?" said Skip. "I haven't met him."

I pointed out Mac, who was over at the volleyball net on the other side of the bonfire.

"Sort of an Attila the Hun type, isn't he?" said Skip.

Allen shot him a warning glance. "Hasn't the lady just said he's a friend of her brother's?" he said.

"Mac is a very nice guy," I said, firmly fixing Skip with a look.

"Excuse me!" said Skip, ironically, lifting his orange drink can. "I think I'll just, uh, freshen my drink."

"Sometimes I can't think how you stand him," I said, after Skip had left.

"Oh, Skip's all right," said Allen. "You just have to know how to take him."

"He's his own worst enemy," said Mona. I stared at her. I couldn't believe she had said that. Next she would be saying, "It takes all kinds."

"After all," she said, "it takes all kinds."

"I better go find Mac," I said. "I don't want him to feel deserted. He doesn't know anybody here."

When I got back to the group with Mac in tow, Skip had returned, and Art and Lindsay had joined them. I introduced Mac to everybody. Allen suggested we bring our hot dogs over so we could all eat together. I appreciated his efforts to make Mac feel at home. Lindsay was so gaga over Mac, and Art was so gaga over Lindsay, that despite their good intentions they were sort of out of touch with the social situation and not much help.

Later, when we all gathered around, carrying hot dogs in various stages of drippiness, Allen made the effort to carry on polite chitchat with Mac, which I thought was sweet of him. Once or twice I did get this eerie feeling that Mac was going to tell a funny story about when I was a little girl, but fortunately it never happened. I could see that I was a little paranoid about it, and I tried to put it out of my mind.

It should have been nice sitting there by the light of the bonfire listening to the ocean. There I was surrounded by friends, with Mac on one side of me and Allen on the other side, both of them tweaking my toes, looking deep into my eyes, and otherwise making me feel like an attractive girl. Penelope would have loved it. It was like a dream. And yet . . . somehow, already, things were starting to change that night. Partly, I think, it was that people acted differently once Mac had come. When Mac came up with his hot dog, I heard Skip mutter, "Hail the conquering hero." I wondered then if Mac had a bad effect on Skip just because he was so big and kind and sure of himself. Maybe Mac made Skip feel small by comparison.

But I think another part of the change had to do just with me. Mac's being around seemed to fill me with discontent. I wasn't happy anymore. Having him next to me made me realize how much I wanted to matter to him. But as if I didn't want to admit that to myself, I started picking away at what was wrong with other people instead. Mona's conversation grated on me. I felt I couldn't put up with Skip a minute longer. And even Allen, whom I liked so much, came under fire. *If he likes me*, I thought irritably, *why doesn't he tell me so? What's the matter with him?* Luckily, I had too much good sense to let anybody know I was feeling that way, but it drained away the fun I was having in the gang's company. And since I knew I couldn't say what I was thinking, I fell into long silences.

After we ate, we all walked down the beach looking for sea turtles. Lindsay led the trek. Since her father is a marine biologist, she knows everything there is to know about sea turtles and she's very interested in them. But for me it wasn't much fun. Mac politely shortened his stride so we could stay together, and on that long walk down the beach in the moonlight I was right next to him. But I felt worse than I had ever felt at home when I used to peer out the window at him. I think the reason was that at home I had known it was impossible; I would never be anything to Mac but Pearce's little sister. But at Silver Beach I had started thinking of myself as a regular person—a grown-up person. Even Mac seemed to be treating me like an equal. It was the flickering of a feeble bit of hope that was making me so miserable.

Naturally, we never did find a sea turtle. Nothing was going right that night. To my dismay, Mac insisted on walking me home. I had been kind of hoping Allen would walk me back. I figured he'd tell some jokes and tease me a little, and I could go to bed in a happy frame of mind. Instead I got to walk home with Mac and suffer the pangs of unrequited love.

We talked about a lot of things. I even told Mac about my travel plans—about wanting to get out of Fairview and see the world. He probably thought my dreams were pretty childish. I just couldn't get over that to him I was probably still just

Pearce's kid sister. My lovely summer seemed to be falling apart.

The moon was full and like a searchlight in the sky, so it wasn't dark at all, really, just unearthly-looking, with our shadows going ahead of us as we walked back to the MacDougals'. The street was full of shadows where bushes or a bicycle appeared suddenly on the sidewalk ahead of us. Mac was wearing a faded old sweatshirt and white shorts that looked ghostly in the moonlight. I remembered that Pearce had always said the reason Mac was only the second-best swimmer on the team was because of his shape. He wasn't sleek, like Pearce, but bulky, with more resistance in the water. Pearce was kind of a nut about water resistance. One time he had told me I should be glad I was flat-chested because too much bosom cut your time in the water. I went to my room in tears, and Dad had a few words with Pearce about making personal remarks. Another time Mom and Dad had to firmly squelch Pearce's idea of shaving all his hair off to cut his time in the water.

Still, I could see what he meant about Mac. It was true that Mac wasn't sleek. His thighs kind of bulged before tapering to neat kneecaps. I loved the way he looked. *Polly Barron*, I told myself, *if you can get all soppy about a guy's kneecaps, you are absolutely beyond hope.* But I couldn't help it. I liked everything about Mac.

After a while he startled me by saying, "You know back there when you said you wanted to see the world? What sort of thing did you have in mind?"

I had forgotten all about saying I wanted to see the world, but it swept all over me again, the longing to get away, and before I knew it I was pouring out all my ambitions to Mac. Mac has such an attentive way of listening that I could see if I wasn't careful I might end up telling him more than I had meant to. "Travel!" I was saying, "New York City . . . Italy . . . France . . ."

The moonlight shone on the planes of Mac's face as he listened to me very seriously. Then, to my astonishment, he began saying, "I want to see the world, too. What I want is to be where things really happen—D.C. Go to college there. And maybe be a congressman's aide. Learn the ins and outs of politics. Someday maybe run for office."

I was amazed. Mac had never before told me anything that was on his mind. He was usually more of a listener. Not that there was anything very surprising about what he had said. He and Pearce were both really interested in politics and liked to sit around and talk to Daddy about it. Once Daddy helped run the campaign of a friend who was running for state senator, and Pearce and Mac just about went out of their minds with the excitement of it all. The thing that amazed me wasn't that he was interested in politics, but that he was telling me about it.

"I don't want to spend my whole life in Fairview," he said. "I want to do something different."

Well, why not? I thought. Everybody knows that Mac is smart. But I suddenly realized with a little shock that Mac wasn't as self-confident as I had always thought. For just a minute, it was all I could do to keep myself from reassuring him.

I felt that although Mac had been hanging around our house for as long as I could remember, I was just now beginning to understand him. I had never thought to look beyond his friendly personality to wonder what it was he wanted for himself.

We talked a little while longer about growing up in Fairview and how both of us wanted to be sure we saw more of the world before we settled down. Then Mrs. MacDougal came to the door and let me in. She took a good look at Mac and smiled. I wasn't worried about what Mrs. M. would think of Mac. Anybody could tell he was awfully nice. It just shone out all over him.

A little later, when I was getting into bed, I realized it had been a good thing that Mac and I had talked. I was already feeling better. I pulled the sheet up under my chin and decided that if I just thought of Mac as a person and not as some kind of love object or something, then maybe I could be happy having him as a friend.

Later, I realized that it was easier to keep that resolve when I was alone than when Mac was right beside me.

Chapter Five

The next week, during one of the breaks at the pool, Mac dived in and swam a couple of fast laps himself. After watching what passes for swimming at the club pool, it was nice to watch somebody who knew what he was doing for a change. I could tell he didn't have the joy in the water that Pearce did, though. When Pearce is in the water, he looks like an aquatic animal—like something that lives on seaweed and never comes out. With Mac, on the other hand, you get the feeling you're watching some powerful, efficient machine, like a propeller. I was sitting on the side of the pool thinking these things and trying to keep Brian in line when suddenly Mac surfaced right beside me and stood up, pushing his dripping hair out of his eyes.

"Why don't I come by and pick you up for Mona's

pig-pickin'," he said. "You can show me where she lives."
The water streamed in rivulets down his chest. He reached
out to tweak Brian's nose, and I had to hold Brian down to
keep him from engaging in full-fledged combat.

"Sure," I said, feeling a bit confused.

"Say six-thirty?" he said.

I nodded, and with a wave, he was back in the water
swimming over to the lifeguard chair.

"Is break over?" said Brian hopefully.

"Almost," I said. Shortly, from the other side of the
pool, Mac blew the whistle and kids began diving back in
the pool.

"When I grow up, I'm going to be big like Mac," Brian
said positively, making it sound like a career decision.

I got back in the pool to play shark with Brian, but my
mind was a million miles away. Was this a date? I asked
myself. Could it be that Mac enjoyed my company and had
noticed that I was a girl? It was a wonderful idea, and when I
looked at it closely, there was some evidence in support of it.
First, it didn't make much sense for Mac to come by and get
me to show him where Mona lives. Silver Beach is not New
York City, and Mona's house, like everybody else's house, is
pretty easy to find. Also, as she could have told him, her
house is closer to where Mac lives than it is to where I live.
Coming by to pick me up was really going out of his way.
That much was encouraging. But then the black thought hit
me that maybe Mac was coming by to pick me up not because
he enjoyed my company but because Pearce had asked him to
keep an eye on me. That would have been all too typical of
Pearce.

"You're not doing it!" Brian shrieked in my ear. "I told

50

you to pretend I'm a dangerous shark, and you're not doing it.''

I was forced to shelve my serious thinking on the subject until later. Unfortunately, all the serious thinking in the world couldn't shed any light on the matter. I really didn't have any way of knowing whether Mac's stopping by to pick me up for Mona's party came under the heading of romance or was just his usual kindness to small animals and little sisters. I was going to have to wait and see.

That Wednesday afternoon I walked to Beach Boulevard and blew some of my wages on a new dress for the party. I got one almost like the one Lindsay had worn to that first party, a sundress. It looked very pretty on me, I thought, but not so racy as Lindsay's looked on her. No matter how low-cut the dress, it will always look fairly respectable on me. That's just the kind of figure I have.

When Friday night rolled around, I saw that whether Mac thought of this as a date or not, it was pretty clear that Mrs. MacDougal did. She told me she wanted to chat a bit with Mac before I came out. I knew exactly what was going on in her mind because, although Tracy was only two and a half, Mrs. M. had already outlined to me her plans for dealing with her daughter's future boyfriends. ''It's a good thing,'' she said to me once, ''for boys to see that the girl's parents are looking them over. It lets them know they need to shape up and behave.'' Of course, she didn't confess this motive to me when she said she wanted to talk to Mac. She just said sweetly, ''I'd like to get to know Mac a little better, Polly. Why don't you plan to be a couple of minutes late coming out, so we can have time to chat together.''

I didn't like the idea that Mrs. MacDougal was looking Mac over and fixing him with a sharp eye to give him the idea that he should shape up, but I couldn't see any way around it. So that night I sat nervously in my room looking at my watch; I gave her three minutes before I dashed out.

Mac was standing at the door of the kitchen talking to her with his hands in his pockets. I melted at the sight of him. *How could anybody be suspicious of Mac?* I asked myself. He looked so dependable. Mrs. MacDougal must have thought so, too, because when she said goodbye to us, drying her hands on her apron, I noticed she was smiling.

Even though the sun was low in the sky, it was hot to be taking a long walk. It was humid, heavy weather. And I was wearing ballet slippers, not the best shoes for walking. But then, we weren't in any hurry, and Mac kept his hands in his pockets as we made our way in the direction of Mona's house. "Got a letter from Pearce today," he said.

Aha, I thought. And I could imagine what it said: *Are you keeping an eye on Polly?*

"He's getting all his stuff together for the trip," Mac went on. "You wouldn't believe the things they've come up with for backpacking."

"I haven't heard much about what Pearce is up to," I said. It was no accident since Pearce and I didn't write to each other, but Mac couldn't know that. "I've phoned Mom and Dad, but I do most of the talking. I guess he's really looking forward to this trip."

"Oh, yeah," said Mac. "He's gonna love it."

"Pearce always has things his own way," I said suddenly. "Have you ever thought about that?"

Mac looked surprised. "Well, why not?" he said. "We'd all have things our own way if we could."

"Maybe so," I said. "But maybe it's not such a good

52

thing." I paused for a minute, then burst out, "Things are so *easy* for Pearce."

Mac thought about that for a minute. "I don't think he looks at it that way," he said. He thought some more as we walked, then said, "But anyway, that's one of the things I like about Pearce. I mean, there's something you have to like about somebody who breezes along enjoying life and doesn't get all tied up in knots worrying about things. He just takes it for granted that things are going to go his way. I don't know, it's kind of refreshing."

It was certainly a different point of view. There was Mac saying he actually liked it that Pearce was spoiled. Suddenly, I wished I hadn't mentioned Pearce at all. If I had designs on Mac, I should *not* criticize Pearce to him, right? Common sense should have told me that. Sometimes I think I don't have any sense, though, that I am haunted by a ghost, and it's my brother.

Mona's party was the usual crush. Long tables were set up in the backyard for people to eat on, and the staff of Friendly's Barbecue was dishing up plates. Lindsay waved to us as we came up. That meant she had noticed that Mac and I arrived together, which I wasn't sorry about. I could still remember the way Lindsay had looked at Mac when she first met him, and if I could have posted a NO TRESPASSING sign on his forehead, I would have. When we were in line to get to the roast pig, Mac asked Mona's cousin from Cincinnati to sit with us. Of course, this was a sign of Mac's kind heart, since she was looking lost, but it got me down that he was noticing other girls. "Look!" I said. "There are some places over by Allen." I figured that if Mac was going to spend his time talking to Mona's cousin, I could at least talk to Allen.

It was a funny thing, but Mac didn't seem to like Allen. I

couldn't figure it out, because Allen had always gone out of his way to be nice to Mac, but sometimes people are like cats and get their backs up for no reason at all. I was happy to see there was no sign of Skip that night. I found a folding chair and scooted it up next to Allen at the table. On the other side of me, Mac was engrossed in conversation with Mona's cousin, maybe about the scenic wonders of Cincinnati. "Skip didn't make it tonight?" I said to Allen, buttering my roll.

Allen looked uncomfortable and said in a low voice, "He's gone for the rest of the summer."

My heart gave a happy little leap. No more muttered asides. No catty remarks. It seemed too good to be true. But what could be the reason? "Were they only planning to come for part of the summer?" I asked.

Allen murmured almost in my ear, "His mother is very sick."

I realized he was telling me that Skip's mother was dying. Allen was such a lighthearted soul by nature that he just didn't have the equipment to deliver this kind of news; the whole idea made him uncomfortable. My roll fell out of my fingers.

"I knew it would upset you," said Allen unhappily. "Skip and his father didn't want to come at all this summer, but his mother insisted. She's been too sick to come out of the house all summer. They've had a nurse. And last night they had to rush her to the hospital."

It seemed so unreal that here at Silver Beach someone could have been suffering. I felt like such an awful, petty person to have been busy criticizing Skip when he was going through all that. Allen looked away. He really did like for things to stay on the light side. "We ought to send flowers or something," I said.

54

"Yes," said Allen, brightening slightly. "We ought to take up a collection. You know, from Skip's friends."

I felt ashamed that Allen was even including me in the bunch of Skip's friends. I felt like a crummy person from the word go. I was thinking about how I had been complaining to Mac that Pearce was spoiled. Really, how was I so different from Pearce? I hadn't exactly had a hard life, either. I didn't even have problems with my parents the way Lindsay did. Nothing was wrong with my life, except that I was jealous of Pearce. So why was I always feeling so sorry for myself? I got up to get a soft drink to give me time to pull myself together. I fished around a long time in the ice cooler as if I was looking for some particular, weird brand of soft drink, and finally, when my hand was so cold that the circulation seemed to have stopped, I pulled out a can and went back to the table. When I sat down, Allen patted my shoulder. Probably he was thinking that I was a kind, softhearted girl, little knowing what a selfish person I really was.

At that point Mac quit talking to Mona's cousin and shot Allen an unfriendly glance. Nothing Allen did suited Mac. I leaned over toward Mona's cousin. "How do you like Silver Beach so far?" I asked. I intended to redeem myself by being nice to people beginning that very night.

The next afternoon, while I was playing with the kids in the backyard, Lindsay and Ben came over. "Let's take the kids to the park," Lindsay suggested. I went to get the double stroller and to tell Mrs. M. where we were going. Lindsay and I had gotten in the habit of having our heart-to-heart talks on the bench in the park while the kids played, and I knew what this one was going to be about.

Sure enough, no sooner had we sat down than Lindsay said, "Why didn't you tell me Mac had asked you out?"

"He just said he would come by and pick me up for Mona's party," I said. "Would you call that asking me out?"

"Yes," said Lindsay definitely. Lindsay's teeth and the whites of her eyes looked whiter than anybody else's, and her hair looked blonder, because she had such a good tan. I noticed that she moved over to the shady side of the bench and took a small bottle of sun blocker out of her pocket. Even Lindsay had evidently decided that enough was enough. She smoothed a little sun blocker over the bridge of her nose. Noticing me looking at her she said, "I've finished my tan for the summer. Now I just need to maintain it at this level." I realized that if Lindsay approached her future career with the determination and organization she brought to her tan, she was bound to zoom to the top.

"Have you ever thought about what you're going to do for a career?" I said curiously.

"Sometimes I think I might like to be a model," grinned Lindsay. "Daddy would hate that."

"No, seriously," I said.

"Well, seriously, I'll probably end up being a marine biologist, just like my Dad is," she said. "Isn't that grim? And stop trying to change the subject. We haven't gotten at the truth about you and Mac."

I sighed. "Only Mac knows the truth. And I don't have the faintest idea what he's thinking. Sometimes I have the feeling that he's just looking out for me on Pearce's instructions."

"Not likely," said Lindsay. "Did he kiss you good night?"

"No."

"Hmmm."

"You see what I mean?"

"Well, we'll just have to wait and see," said Lindsay. "Maybe he's going to be like Allen and just hang around and blow in your ear."

"That's not Mac's style," I said. "I think Allen is really sort of afraid of girls. Mac isn't like that. I happen to know that back home he dated one of the best-looking, most sophisticated girls in town."

"Hmmm."

I felt more cheerful than I had felt for some time. I was glad Lindsay and I had talked about this. It made me feel I could quit worrying about her flirting with Mac right under my nose. Whatever happened with me and Mac, I felt she was on my side.

The following Monday Mac came by the backyard while Mrs. MacDougal was out shopping. Monday is always the lifeguard's day off, so he had the day free and suggested we take the kids to the beach. At first I felt a little thrill of pleasure that he had come all the way over to the MacDougals' to ask for the pleasure of my company at the beach, but later on I wasn't so sure that I knew what was going on. He seemed so moody and distant. The more I saw of Mac, the less I felt like I knew what he was thinking. On the beach that day, he only seemed to really enjoy himself when he got caught up playing with the kids. Mac really likes kids. Anybody can see that. He rode Brian around on his back, and he taught the twins not to be afraid of the waves. After a while I began to think that it wasn't me that was the attraction, but Mark, Tracy, and Brian.

It was beginning to look as if getting away from home hadn't solved all my problems after all, but had just added to them. I had gotten away from Pearce, all right, but it turned out I carried him along in my head. I couldn't stop thinking about him. And then there was Mac. I had more time alone with him than I'd ever dreamed of back in Fairview. He seemed to like to be around me. But somehow I still ended up feeling as if he wasn't really interested in me. I still felt like a side dish to the main attraction—whether it was Pearce, Mona's cousin, or the MacDougal kids. I wanted some sign that I really mattered to Mac in a special way, just for myself.

Chapter Six

The day after Mac and the kids and I went to the beach, a package arrived from home for me. It was a big brown paper parcel with rows of postage stamps and white labels saying INSURED, and it was stamped all over with block red letters saying FIRST CLASS. *I should wait until tomorrow, my birthday, to open it,* I told myself. But when it came right down to it, I couldn't wait to see what was inside. Back in my bedroom, I tore off the brown paper wrapping, cut through the cardboard box, and pretty soon shredded newspaper was falling all over the floor and little packages spilled out. There was a carefully wrapped little package from Mom and Dad and lots of very sloppily wrapped packages from Pearce that looked like paperback books. I opened the books first. I was really glad to see them because I was desperate for something to read. There were some books that looked funny and a couple that looked serious—a pocket guide to crabs, gulls, and other shore creatures and a battered book by one of my favorite authors, Eloise Hagstaad. It was an early book of hers that I had never read. I couldn't imagine where Pearce had gotten it. I mean, Eloise Hagstaad isn't exactly a household word. He must have spent a lot of time digging up those books and making sure he got ones I hadn't read. It was really awfully sweet of him. I hesitated then, but finally gave in and opened the present from Mom and Dad, too. It was a gold bracelet, a *real* gold bracelet with *14 karat gold* engraved on the inside. Also engraved on the inside was *To Polly on her fifteenth birthday, with love from Mom and Dad.* When you think that you have to pay for engraving by the letter, I was surprised at the length of the inscription. I was even more surprised by the bracelet itself. I couldn't believe they had given me something so expensive and so easy to lose. My parents are not stingy, but they're more inclined to give you something useful, like a nice sweater. They had never given me anything so special for my birthday before. It swept over me all at once—*they miss me.* Suddenly I wanted to be at home so much I could hardly stand it. I wanted to leave right that minute.

Of course, I couldn't leave on such short notice, but that night I did ask Mrs. M. if I could go home the day after my birthday. That was a good time to go, because I knew Mr. MacDougal's vacation was beginning. He would be driving over on Friday and would stay the entire following week. In fact, it would be the perfect time for me to go home for a few days. Mrs. MacDougal agreed, so I called Mom and Dad and told them to expect me on the Friday morning bus. I didn't mention, of course, that I had peeked at their birthday present ahead of time.

The next morning, my birthday, Mrs. M. let me sleep late. I lay in bed for a few minutes after I woke up, thinking about how much more grown-up fifteen sounds than fourteen. I had the idea that when I stepped off the bus at home everybody was going to be dazzled by my maturity. For breakfast, Mrs. M. served me pancakes with candles on them. We had to light the candles three times so each of the kids could have a turn blowing them out, and by then the pancakes weren't exactly hot, but I appreciated the thought.

Except for the breakfast pancakes, it was just a regular day. I had sort of hoped Lindsay might remember that it was my birthday, but I reminded myself that it's easy enough to forget something like that. Of course, it was possible she would bring over a card or something after dinner, I supposed.

By the time we started getting the kids cleaned up for supper, I was beginning to wish that instead of giving me pancakes for breakfast Mrs. MacDougal had given me the day off. I felt kind of frayed around the edges. Mrs. M. was late getting supper ready, so the kids were tired, hungry, and outdoing themselves in pandemonium. From the way they were carrying on, you would have thought they had given up on waiting for the macaroni and cheese and decided to turn cannibal instead.

"Mark has my helicopter!" shrieked Brian. "Make him give it back, Polly!"

"You were playing with his monster, Brian," I pointed out. "Now just let him play with it for five more minutes, and you can have it back. I'm looking at my watch now, just five minutes."

Brian, taking justice into his own hands, grabbed the

61

helicopter and ran into the living room. I had to take it away and give it to Mark. "Now remember, you promised Mark he could play with it when he let you have his monster," I reminded Brian. "Just three more minutes."

Three minutes can be a very long time. At last I transferred the helicopter to Brian's waiting hands, but evidently it had lost its glamor, because then he refused to play with it.

Mrs. M. peeped desperately into the oven. "Just a little while longer," she promised.

Just then there was a knock on the kitchen door. I detached Tracy from my ankle and went to open it. It was Mac! He had his hands thrust in his pockets and he shuffled his feet uncomfortably. "Want to go for a walk?" he asked.

To my astonishment, Mrs. MacDougal encouraged me to go and waved me on. "Think of it as a special bonus," she said. It couldn't have been weirder—Mac appearing on the doorstep before dinner and Mrs. M. urging me to take off while everything was falling apart all around us. But I went. I just hoped I didn't return to find Mrs. M. beating her head against the wall.

We set off walking toward the south end of the island, scattering gulls as we went. I decided it was as if a fairy were looking over my shoulder for my birthday. I had been wishing for time off and—*zap!*—I got time off. I was always wishing to see Mac and—*zap!*—he appeared on the doorstep. Now if I'd had three wishes, the way they do in stories, I'd have one left, so I concentrated on wishing very hard that Mac would turn to me and kiss me. Obviously, though, it was real life and not a fairy story at all, because he didn't kiss me. He didn't even look at me, and he didn't say much. In fact, it was a kind of depressing walk. We walked along the sand dunes, because the tide was in and you couldn't walk on the beach. I figured it would have made a good commercial for iron tonic. Camera flashes to couple with slumped shoulders struggling through the sand dunes. Deep voice intones: "Feel tired? Worn down? Depressed? Take Vigoroo!"

I told Mac how I was planning to go home over the weekend. "Do you think you could get off this weekend and go, too?" I said. "The bus trip wouldn't seem so long if I had somebody to talk to." He didn't even stop to consider it, but just flat out said no. That kind of hurt my feelings. One thing was certain. Either he really didn't want to go home or else he really didn't want to go with me. *Why did Mac come to get me at all?* I asked myself. *Isn't he going to say anything?*

At last we turned around and trudged back in the other direction. In spite of my misery and my thinking this was an awful birthday, I began to wonder if something was bothering Mac. Maybe he'd *wanted* to talk, but I had been so wrapped up in myself and full of self-pity that I hadn't made him feel he could tell me what was on his mind. *Polly strikes out again*, I thought. But soon we were back at the house, and it seemed too late to invite him to pour his heart out.

We stood at the door awkwardly for a minute or two, then Lindsay stepped out her front door and called to us. However I felt, I could hardly yell, "Get lost," at Lindsay, so we went on over there.

When I stepped in the front door of her house, an avalanche of confetti hit me and everybody screamed, "Surprise!" I was surprised all right. I was so surprised I burst into tears. I had had a pretty hard day, after all. All the gang was there. There was a mound of presents and a cake with fifteen candles, which makes a pretty respectable blaze. Everybody sang "Happy Birthday," and then I blew out the candles. I wished real hard that Mac would be like his old self again. There was a heap of presents, some of them funny and some kind of nice. My favorite was the book Mac gave me, *Around the World in Eighty Days*. It had super pictures and somehow I had never read it. I thought it was sweet of him to remember how much I want to travel, but then Mac always remembers that kind of thing. I wondered if part of the reason he had been acting so strange on the walk was just because the party was cooking back at Lindsay's. It's hard keeping a secret.

"Many happy returns of the day," said Allen formally. Lindsay hugged me. "Happy birthday, Polly," she said. I couldn't believe everybody had gone to all this trouble for me. For a little while I was perfectly happy in that simple way I had been when I first got to Silver Beach.

The next evening, though, when I had finished packing my things, I decided to go by the pool to say goodbye to Mac. I thought about this a long time, because I didn't want it to look as if I was just assuming he'd want to say goodbye to me. After all, if he had been that crazy to say goodbye, he could have come by the MacDougals'. But I decided it would seem perfectly natural for me to offer to bring him something from home.

When I got to the pool, hardly anybody was there, just a couple of men swimming laps. With the big artificial lights shining on it instead of sunshine, the pool looked kind of cold and depressing. Mac was sort of hunched over with his chin in his hands, watching these guys swim. He didn't seem surprised to see me. Feeling self-conscious, I delivered my offer to bring something back for him and told him how long I would be gone.

"Do you have a couple of minutes?" he said. "Maybe we could have a cup of coffee together?"

Now, that was the sort of thing that was so confusing. You'd think that since he had asked me to stay and have a cup of coffee it meant he wanted to talk to me, but when he sat down he didn't say anything. It was like the walk on the sand dunes all over again.

Finally I said, "Is anything wrong, Mac?"

"I've got a problem with Brandon," he said. "I've about decided I can't work with him anymore."

I couldn't believe that. I knew how much Mac had wanted this lifeguard job. He had explained to me that it was very important for him to earn enough money to help pay for his first year of college. But he didn't seem to want to say any more about it.

I realized then that you can get a completely warped impression of someone when you see him around your house for years, playing basketball and football and eating cookies. I had seen Mac around so long that I felt as if I knew him, but actually I didn't have the foggiest idea what was really on his mind. Before that summer, if somebody had asked me what Mac was like, I never would have said he was moody, or that he kept things to himself, or that his mind was full of secret undercurrents. But I was beginning to believe *all* of those things about him.

As I walked the few blocks back to the MacDougals' house, I thought about all that. Sometimes people turn out to have problems you don't understand. (I had problems myself, though I liked to think nobody knew about them.) But even if you don't really understand other people's problems, that shouldn't make you feel like you don't really *know* them. I did know Mac. I had known him for years. I knew how kind he was, how interested in other people. What I should try to do, I decided, was to be a good friend to him, and not act all hurt and offended when he was going through a bad time. (He had said that he wasn't mad at me.) I should believe that and act just the same toward him as usual. After I decided that, I felt a lot better.

The next day on the bus, I sat next to an old lady who told me all about her operations and her grandchildren's divorces. I couldn't wait to get off. I found myself thinking it was too bad Mac didn't find me as easy to confide in as that old lady did.

When the driver opened the doors in Fairview, Daddy was waiting outside with a big hug. We pulled my suitcase off the luggage rack and headed for the car. I was glad to avoid going into the station, because I have noticed that bus stations are generally full of the weirdest people you can imagine— ladies wearing ostrich plumes on their hats and men who talk to themselves. All in all, although it was very nice to be fifteen, this trip had started me thinking about how much nicer it would be to turn sixteen, get a driver's license, and give up buses for good.

In the car, I showed Daddy I was wearing my new bracelet. "I just adore it," I said.

"That's good, sweetheart," he said. "Mom and Pearce are really looking forward to seeing you."

"I thought Pearce would be gone by now," I said. "Wasn't he supposed to leave last weekend?"

"There's been some holdup," said Daddy. "They had trouble lining up the mules. He's going to fly out the middle of next week. But that's a lucky thing, because now he'll be able to be here the whole time you're home."

I told myself that now that I was bursting with maturity I should be able to handle Pearce, shouldn't I?

When we stepped in the front door, Pearce was waiting and gave me a big hug. Mom came out of the kitchen, drying her hands on a dishtowel, and joined in the hug.

"We've missed you so much, Polly," she said. "It makes me just dread the time you and Pearce go away to school."

It seemed to me a little early to be dreading that. It would be eons before *I'd* be going off to school. But it was nice to know I was missed.

"I'm going to grow a beard while I'm out in Colorado," said Pearce. "What do you think?"

Mom rolled her eyes and headed back to the kitchen. I could tell this had been a subject of discussion before. "I think it sounds like a good idea," I said. It would probably be good for his character, I thought. Maybe with his handsome face covered up by a scraggly beard he'd find out who loved him for himself alone.

I followed Mom into the kitchen. She was dropping balls of dough for cheese puffs onto cookie sheets. "The Japanese beetles have been perfectly horrible this summer," she said. "They ate all the Shasta daisies up before they even got a chance to bloom. All that was left were these silly yellow buttons without a petal to their name."

"Sounds awful," I said sympathetically. It was as if I had never left home. Nothing had changed. It was summer, so naturally Mom's battle with the insects was on.

"Polly," Dad called from the hall. I went out into the hall and suddenly saw there was a birthday cake in the living room, all glowing with fifteen candles. Mom, Dad, and Pearce gathered behind me and started singing "Happy Birthday," slightly off key.

67

It felt awfully good to be home. As glad as I was that I had gone to Silver Beach for the summer, I was even gladder that I could come home to Mom, Dad, and Pearce anytime I wanted to.

"Blow out the candles, Polly," said Pearce impatiently. "Are you asleep or something?"

"Leave her alone, Pearce. It's her cake," said Dad.

Honestly, *nothing* ever changed at home.

Chapter Seven

I got back to Silver Beach at lunchtime on Wednesday. Mrs. MacDougal was obviously almost as glad to see me as Mom and Dad had been. I got the feeling that the MacDougals had had as much family togetherness as they could stand. As we drove from the mainland bus station back over to Silver Beach, Mrs. MacDougal filled me in on their immediate plans. "Tonight we're going out to dinner with friends," she said. She didn't quite burst into joyful song at that point, but it sounded as if she might. "I think Jack is ready for some adult conversation for a change," she went on, "and I know I am."

I carried my suitcase into the house, where I was greeted warmly by Mr. MacDougal. The twins hid behind him as if they had already forgotten who I was, but Brian remembered me perfectly well and tried to punch me in the stomach. I blocked him neatly with my suitcase and announced I would have to unpack.

As I carefully stowed away my hairbrush and T-shirts in my dresser drawers, I wondered if Mac had missed me while I was gone. Not very likely, I decided. I was only away for four days, after all. He probably hadn't even noticed I was gone.

As soon as I got everything put away, I volunteered to take the kids to the park. It turned out that Lindsay and Ben were able to go with us, which was nice. Mr. and Mrs. MacDougal stood in the doorway with their arms around each other and beamed as we left. "We'll be gone about an hour," I called to them.

When we got to the park, Lindsay caught me up on what had happened while I was gone. "You'll never guess what's happened," she said. "Allen is going with Mona."

I felt a little twinge of jealousy. "You mean they are actually dating?" I said in disbelief.

"Of course not. Allen never *dates* anybody. You know that. He's just hanging around. But Mona is ecstatic. She's always been crazy about Allen."

I couldn't really quite imagine Allen liking Mona. He was a pretty clever guy. Did he really want to hear about Mona's Princess telephone?

"I think Allen has decided that you and Mac are a permanent pair," Lindsay went on.

"I wish I was as sure of that as he is," I said.

"Well, you know how Mac looks daggers at Allen every time he comes near you. I guess it started to get on Allen's nerves. Mac can look pretty threatening."

"It's funny how they don't get along," I said.

"Oh, I don't think it's so funny," said Lindsay. "Two guys, one girl."

I thought about how generous Lindsay was. You never saw any sign of envy in her. Here she was saying that Allen and Mac were both interested in me, and she actually seemed pleased for me. *I'd like to be a generous person like Lindsay,* I thought. "You know, Lindsay," I said, "sometime I'd like you to meet my brother." At first I couldn't believe I was saying it. Here was a friend of mine who hardly even knew Pearce existed, and here *I* was setting myself up—actually setting myself up on purpose—to be a stepping-stone to Pearce.

"Your brother?"

I had kept so quiet about Pearce she had probably forgotten he existed. "Yes. You know. Mac's friend. My brother. Pearce." I said patiently. "Maybe you can come up to Fairview some weekend this fall and stay with me. You could meet my family."

"I'd like that," said Lindsay, smiling.

That was a sort of turning point for me. Maybe I was really getting on top of this Pearce thing at last.

That night, according to plan, Mr. and Mrs. MacDougal went out to dinner. Brian had taken an afternoon nap, unusual for him, and I expected him to try to stay up late, but instead, he fell asleep again as soon as they left. That should have pleased me, but it didn't. It worried me. I went up and sat by his bed to watch him. He had a little bit of a cough and a touch of sniffles. But what bothered me was that he had seemed so tired. I noticed that there were blue circles under his eyes. I reached out and felt his forehead. I was afraid it

71

would be hot, and it was. He stirred at my touch and woke up.

"I want Mommy," he said.

"She'll be home later, sweetheart," I said.

"I want Mommy now," he whimpered. A tear streamed down his cheek. I went to get the thermometer. Since he was awake, that was the best time to find out exactly how hot he was. "Now, you must keep this in your mouth until I tell you," I said, holding it steady with one hand while I followed the second hand on my watch. Brian didn't complain about the thermometer once during the three minutes it was in his mouth, which was another thing that worried me. It wasn't like him. I took it over to the doorway where my back would be to the light and checked the thin gray line of mercury. It read 102. That wasn't so good. Oh, how I wished the MacDougals were home.

"When is Mommy going to be home?" said Brian.

"I'm not sure, sweetheart," I said. "But I'm going to try to find out." I went downstairs and pulled down the telephone number that Mrs. MacDougal had clipped to the refrigerator with a magnet. I'd tell Mrs. MacDougal what Brian's temperature was and let her tell me what to do. I called the restaurant and asked for the MacDougals. After I had described what Mrs. MacDougal was wearing, the person who had answered went to look for them.

"There's nobody here of that description," she said when she returned.

"Are you sure?" I said.

"Maybe they've already left," she said.

I glanced at the clock. It was nine o'clock. They had only

been gone for an hour. They certainly couldn't be coming home already.

I thought I could hear Brian starting to cry upstairs.

"Thank you," I said and hung up.

Just then the phone rang again. *Maybe it's the MacDougals,* I thought, relieved. *They've gone to a different restaurant, and they're calling to tell me the new phone number.*

But it was only Mac.

"Mommy!" Brian cried upstairs.

"Oh, Mac, I can't talk now," I said desperately. "Something is wrong with Brian."

Now that I realized I couldn't reach the MacDougals, I began to feel really frightened. If only they had a local doctor, someone I knew and could call up at night the way I would have done at home.

I ran upstairs to Brian. He was wide-awake, but he looked like he didn't have the energy to raise a finger. He gave a little cough. To somebody who knew what Brian was usually like, it was scary. I thought of giving him aspirin, but then I remembered reading somewhere that sometimes aspirin wasn't a good thing. Maybe it's the flu, I thought. But somehow what Brian had didn't seem like flu, and didn't seem like a cold.

"I'm going to sing you a song, Bri, O.K.?"

He didn't say no, so I began singing softly, and after a while he dropped off to sleep again.

A few minutes later, I heard a noise downstairs. *They're home!* I thought, jumping up and running to the head of the stairs. But it wasn't the MacDougals. It was Mac.

"Oh, Mac," I wailed. "I wish the MacDougals were here."

Mac ran up the steps to take a look at Brian. I could tell he was worried, too, because he offered to go get them for me. It seemed like an eternity since they had left, and I began to think they might have left the restaurant and gone to the house of those friends of theirs for coffee or something. Mac said he'd bike over to Beach Boulevard and case the restaurants. Really, by that time I was feeling so panicky I couldn't see straight, but Mac reached out and touched me gently, and that actually calmed me down. I wondered how I could have ever thought Mac didn't care about me. He did. Just for a minute I felt very quiet, as if everything was going to be all right.

After Mac left, I went back up and sat by Brian's bed to watch him breathe. I had no idea what I would do if he stopped breathing, but it was a comfort to me to see his chest moving up and down. I just hoped that Mac would find his parents and that soon I could hand the responsibility over to them.

It seemed like forever, but it must not have been very long before the MacDougals got back. Mac had found them. An overwhelming sense of gratitude swept over me as they came thundering up the stairs and dashed into Brian's room.

Once they were there, I felt embarrassed for causing so much commotion. "I would have called you," I said apologetically, "and just asked you what you thought, but you weren't at that restaurant. I didn't know what else to do but send Mac. I didn't know whether I should give Brian aspirin or not. He's got a temperature of 102."

"That could be serious," said Mr. MacDougal. We were standing out in the hall. "How did he seem?"

"That's what bothered me," I said. "He seemed so tired and listless. Not like himself at all."

"Maybe it's bronchitis," said Mrs. M. "I've seen him get

that way with bronchitis. I'll take him in to the doctor tomorrow.''

''We'll just put a cot in his room tonight so one of us can sleep with him and keep an eye on things,'' added Mr. M.

I still felt a little bit silly having called them home, but I also felt tremendously relieved. As soon as Mrs. M. said bronchitis, I felt much better. Just giving the sickness a name made me feel better.

The next morning, Mrs. MacDougal drove Brian to the mainland to see a doctor Mrs. Ellis had recommended. She told me later that he had no sooner put the stethoscope to Brian's chest than he said, ''Pneumonia.'' Mrs. M. had nearly passed out. It turned out to be what they call walking pneumonia, which means, I guess, that you aren't so bad off that you can't get around. He put Brian on antibiotics and prescribed bed rest for a week. Mr. and Mrs. MacDougal felt I had been very smart to see that something was really wrong, and I figured that at least I had learned a rule I could keep in mind for the future—if a kid seems really sick, he probably is.

Our next problem was to entertain Brian while he spent a week in bed. Lindsay's mother brought over some of Ben's puzzles, and we stocked up on books, but when you have to entertain a kid from dawn to dark, the day seems to have an awful lot of hours in it. What a relief when Brian was finally allowed to go out and play! I never thought I would actually be looking forward to watching him run around hitting people in the stomach, but I was.

The next night Evie Turner had a luau, and since I had spent the entire week reading aloud from things like *A Child's History of Trucks* and *The Adventures of Benjamin Bunny*, I felt I really deserved a party. Lindsay lent me a sarong for the occasion. It looked very Hawaiian. I only hoped it would stay up all evening. I had a horror of something coming untied and the whole thing slipping gently to the ground, but Lindsay said not to be silly and that nobody double-knots sarongs.

When Mac and I got to Evie's, we were given leis, but Mac took the first opportunity to ditch his. "You wear it," he said, draping it over my head. "It makes me feel like a blinking Christmas tree." Colored lights had been strung all over the yard. If you looked at them closely, they looked like the same colored lights that had been at Miranda's party. In the center of the yard, on a pit over hot coals, was a whole roast pig with an apple in its mouth. It could have been the same roast pig that had been at Mona's pig-pickin'. I could tell Evie had gone to a lot of trouble to give the party a Hawaiian flavor. There were pineapples cut lengthwise laid out on the serving tables and a loudspeaker was playing island music, but still, it was as if the party were made up of bits and pieces of parties we had already been to. Not that I minded. I kind of liked the familiar feel. Mac gave me a friendly squeeze. "Another Silver Beach bash," I said happily. "I love 'em."

The thing about parties is that it isn't the decorations that matter but the people. If Evie had served up a bowl of soggy potato chips and a washtub of Kool-Aid, I would have been just as happy, because I was there with Mac and he was back to being his old self again. I knew I might never find out what it was that had been going on with Mac and Brandon, but Brandon had suddenly disappeared from the pool and Mac was walking on air. So I knew that whatever that war had been about, Mac had won it.

Also, I felt better myself. Not only did I feel like I was

76

finally rising above my problems with Pearce, but ever since the awful night that Brian had been so sick and Mac had come running to my side to help, I felt sure that whether he ever kissed me good night or not, he cared what happened to me.

"I've never been to so many parties in my whole life," said Mac thoughtfully. "I think there's been a party almost every single weekend I've been here."

I thought about it and decided he was right. "I think it's nice," I said. "You couldn't keep up this pace at home where you have to stay on top of the algebra or whatever, but it makes for a terrific summer."

"Have you ever thought about what these things must cost?" said Mac.

I didn't like to admit it, but I hadn't.

"These summer houses on the beach and the country club, too," he said. "Those things are awfully expensive."

I wasn't sure what he was getting at. "You think parties are extravagant?" I asked.

He looked thoughtful. "Well, I don't feel like Evie's awful to have a party. And I like going to them," he said, "but I guess it does make me feel a little bit funny. When you think of all the people in the world who are really poor, like the people my mom works with, it seems kind of funny that we're here stuffing ourselves with roast pig."

I could see what he meant. Sometimes Mac makes me feel very shallow.

"You're not going to ruin this party for me, are you, Mac?" I said.

"I'm not trying to," he protested.

"What do you want for dessert, sherbet or two-finger poi?"

"Sherbet," he said with feeling, "definitely."

We got up to go toward the serving tables. I wondered what Evie was going to do with all the leftover two-finger poi.

Chapter Eight

Once Mac had pointed out to me the economics of parties, I realized that a beach party was a low-budget deal. The only expenses were quantities of hot dogs, potato chips, soft drinks, and wood for the fire. And I actually got to where I liked beach parties best, because after Mac laid the moral view of parties on me, a live band just reminded me of the starving poor in Afghanistan.

For me, the best party of all was Bobby Sherridan's beach party. I liked it best because that was the night Mac finally kissed me. At first things didn't look promising. We had barely finished our hot dogs when a large drop fell on my nose. I heard a sizzling sound as some raindrops hit the hot logs of the fire. Bobby walked passed me, saying hopelessly, "I knew it. I just knew it. The minute I have a party, it's got to rain." All around us people were squealing,

"It's raining!" and, "It's started to rain. Let's get out of here." Mac scrambled up. "I better help Bobby stow away all this stuff," he said. "It looks like it's really going to come down."

There wasn't any place on the beach to take cover, so I just stood there hugging myself while the rain came down. Everyone ran like mad for home except Bobby, Mac—the good Samaritan—and me. *Well,* I told myself, *one of the things you like about Mac is that he's such a nice guy, and it* is *nice of him to want to help Bobby.*

It was a warm night, but those raindrops were cold. That made for an interesting sensation as they slowly dripped down my neck. I heard distant thunder as Mac helped Bobby load up the serving table and the ketchup bottles. The fire kept burning in the rain, but I didn't figure it would last long. I knew that I, for one, was getting quickly extinguished.

Bobby wrung Mac's hand. "Thanks a lot, Mac, old buddy," he said. "I really appreciate it." Then he turned his collar up, jumped in his car, and roared away without offering us a ride.

Mac looked at me, and we both burst out laughing. "I think Bobby is kind of rattled," I said. It wasn't really very far to the MacDougals' and we were already wet anyway, so there was no point in getting upset about it. Mac's arm felt very warm when he put it around me, and we started walking. The water on the streets sloshed in my sandals and made them slippery inside, so I stopped to take them off and hang them over my arm. I could feel the street, wet and gritty under my feet.

"One thing about the rain," said Mac, wiping the water off his face, "you have a lot of privacy."

"What?" I said. The rain was coming down so hard now it

was making a kind of swooshing noise and spattering on the pavement, so I couldn't hear him too well.

Then he bent over, put both arms around me, and kissed me. After that I wouldn't have noticed a tidal wave. I felt I had been waiting for that moment a long time.

In just a few more minutes, we made it home, and Mrs. M. met us at the kitchen door. "Goodness," she said, appalled. "You two look like drowned kittens. Come in and dry off, Mac."

"I don't want to drip on your floor," said Mac.

"Just stand over there in the corner," said Mrs. M. She disappeared in the direction of the linen closet and came back with two huge bath towels for us. I blotted my dripping hair, and Mac wiped his face off.

"We got caught in the rain," I said.

"I guessed that," said Mrs. M. dryly. "Let me run you home, Mac," she said.

"Aw, I'm already so wet there's no point in it," he said. "It's not that far." Mrs. MacDougal insisted on his at least taking an umbrella, and he did.

Watching out the front window, I saw Mac and the red umbrella under the streetlight in front of the house, a shower of silver drops falling on him in the halo of light. Then he disappeared into the darkness. I turned back to Mrs. MacDougal. "It was a great party," I said happily, wrapping the towel around me.

"Hmmm," said Mrs. MacDougal, looking at me thoughtfully.

Just a couple of weeks before school started, a cloud appeared on this otherwise perfect picture of happiness. Pearce called Mac and said he wanted to come to Silver Beach for the weekend. Of course, there wasn't any possibility of *forever* hiding from Pearce the fact that Mac and I were going together, but I had been hoping to put off telling him for a couple of weeks longer. I don't know what I expected him to do when he found out, but somehow I knew he wasn't going to like it. Even if he didn't say a word, I figured the look of shock on his face would probably set me back for weeks.

I told Lindsay that Pearce was coming. "Great," she said. "Maybe I'll get a chance to meet him while he's here." I didn't say anything. Of course, I should have been plotting to throw Lindsay and Pearce together. Not only did I owe it to my friend Lindsay, who must have had a pretty blah summer, but I also owed it to myself, if I didn't want to end up with somebody like Leila for a sister-in-law. There was still time to open Pearce's eyes to the idea that there were girls who had more to offer than simpering sweetness. But I couldn't think of that just then. I was dreading Pearce's getting there too much.

"Don't you want him to come?" said Lindsay, puzzled.

"Pearce has been away in Colorado," I said. "He doesn't have any idea that I'm seeing Mac."

"But I thought you said Mac was his best friend."

"It's hard to explain, Lindsay, but take it from me, he's not going to like it. The thing is, Pearce thinks Mac hung the moon, while he sees me more as a lovable three-year-old idiot. He's going to figure Mac's crazy."

Lindsay was still puzzled. "What difference does it make what he thinks? He's not involved."

She was right, of course, and yet . . . "The thing is," I said, struggling to explain, "Pearce is a . . . well, he's been my big brother my whole life."

Lindsay snorted. "If you let what your brother thinks ruin

your chances with Mac, you *will* be acting like a three-year-old idiot.''

''Oh,'' I said hastily, ''what Pearce thinks doesn't matter a flip to me. It's just that it's going to be so . . . weird at first.'' And it turned out that on that score I was absolutely right.

Pearce was supposed to arrive Friday afternoon. He and Mac were to come by and pick me up for a movie after supper. Going over the bridge to the mainland for a movie would be a special treat for us. At least that was the way it was supposed to work. At seven-thirty, just as planned, Pearce and Mac pulled up in front of the MacDougals' house in Mom's little Plymouth, and Mac jumped out to open the door for me. From the way Pearce looked at him, it was perfectly plain that he expected me to open my own doors. And besides, he was expecting me to sit in the backseat.

''How was Colorado?'' I asked, after I had squeezed in between the two of them on the front seat. I noticed there was no sign of a beard. I supposed Pearce had decided not to take the risk of letting people love him for himself.

''Fantastic!'' he said. ''You gotta go out there sometime. You won't believe it. At first I had a lot of trouble getting my breath at that altitude. But after a while I got used to it, and everything was fine. Out on the peaks we'd see these Dall sheep, you know, the ones with the big, curvy horns. Then there were these cute little critters called pikas that would call to each other like they were sending telegraphs—*click, click, click*. The thing about climbing,'' Pearce went on ecstatically, ''is that you have to completely trust your partner. One false move, and *wham!*—it's curtains for you both.''

I noticed that this was a slightly different version of the trip than had been given to Mom and Dad when Pearce was trying to sell them on the idea. If I remembered right, what we had

had heard about then was the "supervision by trained instructors."

Three people in a front seat can be pretty crowded when one of them is as big as Mac. Mac shifted around uncomfortably, then put his arm around me. At that point, Pearce paused in his description of the thrills of mountain climbing and looked at Mac's arm as if it were a boa constrictor.

In the movie, Mac and I held hands. We were trying to act as natural as possible, but it wasn't easy. I was sitting between Mac and Pearce, and at first I don't think Pearce even noticed that Mac and I were holding hands. But when he decided to go out and get popcorn, he saw, and the expression on his face made him look like a character from some old-fashioned play. You expected him to jump up and bellow, "Unhand my sister, sir!" When he got back with his popcorn, he shot us a thoughtful glance. I guess there have been times I have been more uncomfortable in my life, but not more than once or twice.

When we got back to the MacDougals' after the movie, Mac walked me up to the door. I saw him glance involuntarily back at the car where Pearce was waiting. If he had shaken hands with me I wouldn't have blamed him. Instead he gave me a fast peck on the forehead. "Night, Polly," he said.

This is awful, I thought. *I can't stand it two more days.* The funny thing was, though, that the next day was much better. Mrs. M. encouraged us all to go to the beach together, and I invited Lindsay to come along. That turned out to be a big help.

For one thing, Lindsay acted perfectly normal. That meant one person out of four was acting normal, which was an improvement. And then, Lindsay and Pearce kind of hit it off, which meant Pearce had something else to do besides glare at

Mac and me. At one point Lindsay took Pearce off to look for ghost crabs. They were both really interested in crabs. Mac and I stayed behind. Lindsay had shown me some ghost crabs one time, and I felt like once was enough. (They are so transparent that all you see about them at first is their black dots of eyes. To put it mildly—they are definitely not as cute as kittens.) But Pearce is never happier than when he's peering closely at some boring mollusk or looking through binoculars at some obscure splash in the water that might turn out to be an otter. Mac and I sat on the beach and waited for them to get back. "I think Pearce was a little bit surprised that we're going together," said Mac.

"He seems to be getting used to the idea," I ventured.

Shortly, Pearce and Lindsay reappeared and threw themselves down on the sand beside us. "Lindsay says you can keep hermit crabs as pets," announced Pearce. *No thanks,* thought I. Those weird claws of theirs going *scritch scratch* as they scuttle across the floor. I'll stick to things with warm blood.

"My cousin sent me some in the mail from Florida one time," said Lindsay. "They can go without food and water for a week, so they're easy to mail." I could imagine the feelings of the postman delivering a package with mysterious scurryings inside. It didn't bear thinking about.

I was glad when Pearce headed back to Fairview. There was only a tiny scrap of summer left and I wanted to enjoy it without his being around. Seeing him had made me realize how near it was to the time to go home. From then on, every time Mac and I took a walk on the beach I felt I was storing up a memory in my heart for the long winter.

I realized I was really dreading going home. It wasn't easy

to say why. Mac would still be there. And I really love my family. I suppose I was just afraid that what I had gotten during the summer would somehow manage to slip out of my hands. At Silver Beach I felt like an independent person. I wasn't sure that feeling could be packaged safely and brought home.

The last afternoon I was at Silver Beach, Mac and I took a long walk. It was a beautiful afternoon, blue water, gold sunshine sparkling on it, and everything feeling the way things do when you know they aren't going to last too long. Mac was on top of the world thinking about his senior year and how he could probably go to college where he wanted to, at Georgetown. He squeezed me close and kissed me. No cloud was on his horizon. But for me it wasn't so simple. I didn't have his confidence that things would go on being so good. As we walked, we stirred up a flock of laughing gulls. They circled over our heads chuckling. Of course, that's just the way laughing gulls always sound, but it seemed to me as if they were laughing at me, as if they were saying, "Ha, ha, now you see us, now you don't." Then they vanished away in the sky like the summer.

It's lucky that things don't always turn out as awful as you think they might. When I actually got home, things weren't bad at all. It turned out I had been able to transport my self-confidence home after all. I still had the problem of my friends being fascinated with Pearce and his gang, but somehow I had gotten to where I could see the funny side of that. And Pearce seemed to realize that I wasn't a little girl any more. He even accepted that Mac and I were a couple. Except for driving me crazy holding the phone out of my reach when Mac called, Pearce didn't give me any more trouble. I saw that I had been wrong when I said that nothing ever changed at home. *I* had changed, and that was enough. Everything seemed to go more easily for me.

Mac and I went together to the big get-acquainted party the school throws in the fall to welcome incoming freshmen. I noticed all the poor freshmen gathered together in clumps along the wall, probably wishing they were dead. I felt sorry for them. I couldn't help but be glad not to be a freshman anymore. I figure your embarrassment quotient drops ten percent for every year you're older. Look how much a single summer had done for me. Last year I had been just as embarrassed as they were. In fact, I couldn't tell you anything about last year's get-acquainted party because my memories are all blurred by a pink haze of embarrassment. I had been too worried that I was going to trip and do a nose dive into the punch bowl to notice much about what was going on. But this year I could actually look around and see what other people were doing.

I saw Pearce and Nancy Jane Patterson floating past a bank of tissue paper flowers. They made a beautiful couple—gorgeous matching blonds. I wasn't the only person who noticed them. Mr. Elwood, the bald music teacher, was eyeing them as they passed him. I supposed that when you got to where you were losing your hair, like Mr. Elwood, you must wonder whether all the experience and wisdom in the world were a fair trade for looking as gorgeous as Nancy Jane and Pearce. I said something like that to Mac, but he snorted, "Mr. Elwood never looked like Pearce in his life. He's probably always looked just like Mr. Elwood." I didn't think it was very likely that Mr. Elwood had been bald and wrinkled at eighteen, but I didn't want to argue about it.

A freshman couple bumped into us and turned red all over. They were so shaken that they stopped in their tracks and disappeared from the dance floor.

"Do you ever think about the kids at Silver Beach?" I asked.

"Nope," said Mac. "Hardly ever think about them."

"I do," I said. It had been a big summer for me, a very growing-up kind of summer. I knew I would never forget it. "You know Lindsay's coming to spend the weekend next month," I added.

"That's nice."

"Yep. Pearce is going to try to persuade her to hike the Appalachian Trail next summer."

Mac grinned. We headed toward the punch bowl together. A cafeteria table had been covered with a white tablecloth and decorated for the party by the Home Ec classes. They had also baked pounds and pounds of brownies for the occasion. In the center of the table was a nice arrangement of daisy chrysanthemums. Mac sneakily picked one of the flowers and started pulling the petals off. "She loves me, she loves me not," he began gravely. Then he pulled the last petal off. "She loves me not?" he said, looking at the last petal with blank astonishment.

"What does a flower know?" I said, taking his hand and leading him back to the dance floor. "You should ask *me.*"

He put his hand around my waist and grinned at me as we started to dance. "That's all right," he said. "I can read minds."

To read Mac's side of this story, flip this book over and begin reading on page 1.

About the Author

Janice Harrell decided she wanted to be a writer when she was in the fourth grade. She grew up in Florida and received her master's and doctorate degrees in eighteenth-century English literature from the University of Florida. After teaching college English for a number of years, she began to write full time. Her Archway titles include: *FLASHPOINT* and *THE MURDER GAME*. She has also written two books for younger readers: *TIFFANY, THE DISASTER* and *THE GREAT EGG BUST*, both available from Minstrel Books.

She lives in Rocky Mount, North Carolina, with her husband, a psychologist, and their daughter. Ms. Harrell is a compulsive traveler —some of the countries she has visited are Greece, France, Egypt, Italy, England, and Spain—and she loves taking photographs.

EVERY LOVE STORY HAS TWO SIDES

MAC'S STORY . . .

It was natural when you thought about it, that your best friend and your girlfriend might come from the same family. But it was a heck of a disadvantage too, and it took me quite a while before I could kick this hallucination that Pearce was following us everywhere.

Mac is starting the summer job he dreamed about as head lifeguard at Silver Beach. He's away from home for the first time. And he's not alone. Polly Barron is there too, but she's his buddy's kid sister. She looks a lot older out at Silver Beach and just as grown up as the girls that Mac is used to dating. Only a lot more special. Now Mac has two problems: Can he make Polly realize that he wants to be more to her than Pearce's buddy? And how is he ever going to explain to Pearce that he's fallen hard for Polly?

TWO BY TWO ROMANCES™ are designed to show you both sides of each special love story in this series. You get two complete books in one. Read what it's like for a boy to fall in love. Then turn the book over and find out what love means to the girl.

Mac's story begins on page one of this half of *One Special Summer*. Does Polly feel the same way? Flip the book over and find out.

More Two By Two Romances™
from WARNER BOOKS

5

TWO BY TWO
ROMANCE™

One Special Summer

Janice Harrell

WARNER BOOKS

A Warner Communications Company

One Special Summer

MAC'S STORY

Chapter One

It was the worst Tuesday night in our family's history. We all sat down with a blue spiral-bound notebook in which my mother and father had recorded every penny we'd spent for the past six months, and we tried to figure out where we could cut. Since we hadn't exactly been living like the Royal Family to begin with, I didn't feel there was a lot of hope.

Mom wrinkled her brow. "What's this in February? Two hundred dollars for Miscellaneous?"

"I just couldn't account for every penny, that's all," said Dad, snapping his pencil in two with annoyance.

"We'll just have to keep better records from now on," said Mom. "Now here's an item we can cut. Food. It seems incredible that we could spend that much on food."

Mom's and Dad's eyes crept in my direction. I'm a big guy and I do eat a lot. It was beginning to sound more like Hansel

and Gretel every minute. I cleared my throat uncomfortably. Their eyes moved back to the blue notebook. "Of course, we have to have enough to eat," Mom said, as if she was unwilling to admit it. "All I mean is that we can probably save money by clipping coupons and not buying prepared foods. I'll have more time for cooking now."

My mother's job as a social worker had just come under the cost-cutting ax. She would be laid off as of July. That meant the job would last long enough to see my brother Leo through college—he got out in June—but in a little over a year I'd be going myself, and that was what had us worried.

Mom raised her pen to the paper hopefully. "Now, don't you think we can figure to save ten percent on food?" she asked.

"Sure," said Dad.

"I hate to mention it," I said, "but what about inflation?"

They looked at me as if I'd invented it.

Mom sighed. "Mac's right," she said. "Let's figure a savings of four percent."

Great. At that rate we'd have my spare shoelaces paid for in no time.

"What about Christmas presents?" I said. "That's a pretty big item. We don't have to give each other Christmas presents."

"That's easier to say in March than in November," Dad said. "I speak from experience."

"Besides," said Mom, "we mostly give you and Leo clothes, which you need anyway, and where else are we going to cut down? Old great-aunt Ethel, whose only joy is hearing from us? Grandma?"

I could see the problem.

2

"I'm getting a headache," said Mom. "Maybe we can work on this some more tomorrow."

Dad picked up the budget. "Don't worry, Ruth. We'll manage somehow. If the transmission holds up, the car ought to last for two more years." (My father already drives the oldest car in the DA's office.) "And if we come up short, Mac will just have to borrow some money to see himself through school. But I don't think it will come to that. I'm pretty sure if we watch our pennies we can get him through State. Don't forget, there's always the chance he'll get an athletic scholarship."

Mom brightened slightly. I didn't think this was the time to tell her that I didn't want an athletic scholarship and that I didn't want to go to State.

After we stowed the budget, Dad walked with me down the hall to my room. Mom says Dad and I look a lot alike, and I guess she's right. We both have broad shoulders and bushy eyebrows. He's just a hundred years older and a hundred pounds heavier. He rested a hand on my shoulder. "Don't worry about it, Mac," he said. "We'll manage somehow."

After that I went in my room and worried. From under my mattress, I pulled my savings account book. When I was younger I used to take it out when things got rough, like when my fifth-grade teacher hated me, and figure out how far I could afford to run away. Luckily, things never got rough enough for me to actually use it, because now I needed that money. (I've been more or less socking it away regularly from my summer jobs. It was no secret. Once or twice Dad had said, "What are you doing with the money from that job of yours, Mac?" I'd say, "Saving it," and he'd say, "Good kid." But now it looked like Mom and Dad had forgotten all about my bankbook, because they hadn't mentioned it.) I had

all of fifteen hundred dollars. A few weeks before that had sounded like a lot of money. Suddenly it didn't sound like much.

Mom and Dad didn't realize it, but I had decided to break out of being a jock. I had decided that the same day I decided I didn't want to go to State. It happened last fall when Dad and I stopped off at State to look the place over. We looked up Tootie Johnson, who's the son of a friend of Dad's. He showed us around and took us to his dorm room. While we were walking through the upstairs lounge, I noticed a shattered hulk of a guy sacked out on the couch. He must have weighed three hundred pounds. His knees were wrapped with a few hundred yards of tape, and it looked like somebody had accidentally stepped on his face. "That's Jack McGraw," Tootie whispered reverently as we passed. Of course, I knew who Jack McGraw was. I just hadn't recognized him without the number 12 on his jersey. "Does he ever come to?" I said uneasily.

Tootie looked uncertain about this. "We don't see him around much," he explained. "You know, football practice and everything."

Tootie's dorm room didn't make much of an impression on me—posters on the wall and unmade beds. What did make an impression on me was Jack McGraw. I had heard guys say it was really hard to study when you were on a football scholarship, but it had never hit me what that meant until then. This guy McGraw looked like he had just come in from the war. I couldn't picture him popping up from that coma and hitting the physics book. And what would he have left when he got out of school? Unless he was good enough to go pro, he'd just have his so-so grades and his rotten knees.

It got clearer and clearer to me as I thought about it that I

4

didn't want to end up like Jack McGraw. Another thing, I didn't want to go to State, which was full of people like Tootie Johnson, people I'd known all my life, people who couldn't picture me outside of a football jersey or my swim trunks. The way I looked at it, State could end up being just like high school. What I wanted to do was to make a new start, go to some good college out of state, maybe Washington, D.C., where I could study political science, which interests me more than bashing somebody around on a football field. But the tuition at a place like that would be double what it was at State, and once Mom lost her job, that put me in one heck of a bind.

I figured if I could just get enough money to see me through the first year of school, something might turn up. I knew it was easier for sophomores to get academic scholarships. Also, there was a good chance that by then Mom would have been able to get another job. I was willing to take that gamble. But as worried as Mom and Dad were already, I didn't feel as if I could even talk to them about it until I dug up the difference between what State costs and what some place like Georgetown costs.

One thing I knew. Unless I was going to start manufacturing dollar bills on the little printing press I got when I was seven, I had better get a different summer job. For years and years I'd spent the summer teaching little kids to swim. I didn't exactly teach them to swim. I taught them to put their heads under water, blow bubbles, and kick their way across the pool holding on to a paddleboard. When they could do that, they were ready to graduate into Miss Rigby's class. I liked teaching little kids. That's why I did it. But it isn't a good way to rake in money. Not to say that the pool

management is cheap, but at the last lesson, when the kids dive for pennies, I always have to bring the pennies.

I spent the day after we went over the budget more or less in a daze, the way you do when you're worrying. It was a relief when Mike Christie showed up at my front door that afternoon. "Wanna ride over to Pearce's?" he asked. "Thought we'd shoot a few baskets with Pete and Eric and the guys. How 'bout it?"

In a few minutes a bunch of us were at Pearce's, piling out of the car. I like shooting baskets. Besides, if I don't do a fair amount of running around, I start to get kinks. My favorite sports are football and swimming, but I'll settle for shooting baskets.

The added attraction at Pearce Barron's is his mother's cooking, especially her cookies and cakes. Ever since my mother had been working an eight-hour day, if I wanted something special to eat at our house, I had to defrost some Pepperidge Farm. I like Pepperidge Farm, but they have a long way to go before they match Mrs. B's cooking. I crave those cookies. I eat so much at the Barrons' house they ought to take me off as a tax deduction. That afternoon was no different. We all stuffed ourselves so much we couldn't move enough to keep the game going.

Then Mike said he had to be getting home and everybody piled back into his car.

Pearce said to me, "Stay here. I'll run you home later. I want to show you a book I picked up in Raleigh that's right up your alley."

The rest of the guys left with a roar in Mike's car. He had just gotten the car and wanted the world to know about it. I could see everybody's heads snap back as they tried to avoid whiplash when Mike peeled out of the driveway.

"I wish I had a car like that to abuse," I said.

Pearce went in to get the book, then made his way to the backyard where I was taking in the scenery. Mrs. B.'s a gardening nut, and the yard looks like Eden before the snake hit it—neat rows of flowers all over the place, trees and bushes that look as if a barber trimmed them. Pearce isn't the kind of guy who notices flowers, though, and he managed to grind a daffodil into the ground as he came over to where I was sitting.

He laid a big red-and-blue paperback on my chair. It was a breakdown of every single congressional district in the United States, with an essay on each one telling whether Indians were a big minority group, whether the district ran to smoke-stacks or corn, quirks about the history of the place—all the things that help you figure out who the district is going to vote for. I checked out our district and there we were—small town, tobacco, and textiles, with everybody voting the way they've voted for a hundred years. Then, for contrast, I decided to check out California's eleventh. This was the sort of thing that in normal times I could spend hours doing—reading the rundowns on the districts and looking at the photos of the representatives trying to look honest. I liked to predict the winners of elections and think about how I would have managed their campaigns. But that day, great as this book was, my mind kept trailing back to my troubles.

"I got two of them," said Pearce. "One for me and one for you."

"It's great," I said. "Thanks. I'll pay you for it on Friday, O.K.?"

"Oh, forget it. It was just a few bucks," he said.

"Pearce, I've got to make some money."

He looked startled. I didn't know for sure, but I had the idea that the Barrons didn't have to have a budget. I knew, for

7

instance, that Pearce didn't plan to work this summer at all. He was going to go out West and climb mountains.

"What's the matter?" he said.

"I need more money for college," I said. Then I added, gritting my teeth, "I don't want to go to State."

Pearce is the tall, blond Viking type that girls are always throwing themselves at, but underneath all that he is a heck of a good guy and he didn't laugh.

"What about that job you've got teaching the kids swimming?" he asked.

"Doesn't pay enough," I said. "It's only three mornings a week. I wish I could get a lifeguard job, but in this town those jobs are tied up so tight they might as well be run by the Mafia." In our town the gym teachers skimmed off the cream of the lifeguard jobs.

"Maybe you could get Tom Langard's job," said Pearce. "It turns out he's not going back to that head lifeguard spot at Silver Beach Country Club."

"No kidding?"

"Yep. His parents are giving him a surprise trip to Europe as a graduation present. He just found out. You ought to get in your application now."

The idea sort of took my breath away. Silver Beach was a spot of paradise, a resort town three hours drive from Fairview, a place where kids are willing to kill to get a job picking up cigarette butts, much less being head lifeguard at the country club.

"I'd never get it," I said. "Kids are probably standing in line for it already."

"I told you, Tom's parents just sprung this thing on him," Pearce pointed out. "And don't go putting yourself down. You know Coach would write you a good recommendation.

And don't forget Rigby. She knows you're great with little kids.''

I could already see the gorgeous girls hanging onto my lifeguard chair. I was going into this for money, not fun, but I couldn't help thinking that it sounded like fun.

Pearce's sister Polly came out. ''Mom wants to know if you'd like to stay for dinner, Mac,'' she said. ''There's plenty of pot roast.''

Polly is a cute kid, as good-looking as Pearce in her way, but she was just a freshman then. I could still remember how excited she had been a few years before when her guppy had guppies. Cute.

''Come on and stay,'' said Pearce.

''I'll have to give Mom a call,'' I said, weakening as I thought of Mrs. B's pot roast.

A couple of years ago I would have reached over and tickled Polly, then scooped her up and thrown her over my shoulder. But I was smart enough to know that now she thought of herself as grown up, so I just asked about her research paper. I had given her some books for it a month or so ago.

''It's finished,'' Polly said, pleased. ''Want to read it?''

''Mac doesn't want to read your dumb research paper, for Pete's sake,'' said Pearce.

''No, I'm really interested in Roosevelt,'' I protested.

''You might want to check the mail, Pearce,'' Polly said.

Pearce jumped up like a shot and ran inside. I was glad to see that Polly understood why Pearce was so grouchy. I mean, the way he talked to Polly sometimes, you'd think she was his worst enemy instead of his cute little sister. But he'd gotten moody since Leila moved away. It was one of those weird things. With all the girls that chased Pearce around

9

from morning to night, there was only one girl he'd ever really fallen for, and she had just moved five hundred miles away.

"I'll get you the paper after dinner," said Polly. "Mr. Dixon really liked it. All those books you dug up were a big help."

I thought about how nice it would be to be in Polly's shoes. Life got a lot more complicated when your senior year was almost staring you in the face. Here Pearce was all upset about his girlfriend and here I was worrying myself sick about money for college, but Polly was just bumping along as usual, writing her papers, bringing cookies out to the guys, not a worry in the world. There's a lot to be said for being a kid.

Chapter Two

Swimming practice starts at the crack of dawn and ends just in time for you to shake the water out of your hair and run to homeroom, but Thursday, for some reason, we wound up early. Nobody asked any questions. They just looked at the clock and took off running before Coach changed his mind and ordered us all back in the water. I was stuffing my wet swimsuit into my gym bag as fast as I could when Coach called to me, "Slow down, Mac. Today we're early." He came over and sat down on the bench next to me. "Have you given any thought to college yet?"

"Uh . . . yeah. I've been thinking about it some," I muttered. Actually, I hadn't been thinking much about anything else.

"You might want to talk it over with me before you make up your mind," he said. "I'd be able to help steer you. Now,

you take State. They've got a good swim team, but not so good that you wouldn't be able to stand out, if you see what I mean. That's the sort of thing you need to be thinking about.''

"I don't think I'm going to be on the swim team," I said.

Coach looked disappointed, but not surprised. "Of course, the real money is in football," he admitted.

"Uh . . . I probably won't go out for football, either," I said.

Coach was rocked. Things were worse than he had imagined, but he was still determined to help. "Are you having troubles at home, kid?" he said gently. He obviously figured if I was thinking of giving up sports, I must really be cracking up under some strain.

"No, everything's fine at home," I said.

"Well, if you're not going to play football and you're not going to swim, what are you going to do in college?" he asked.

I zipped up my gym bag. "Study," I said.

"But your grades are always good," he said. "You're one I never have to worry about there."

"High school is one thing," I said. "But in college I'll be up against some real competition." I propped my foot on the bench to tie my sneaker. "It's different for me than for the other guys," I said, trying to explain. "I'm good at sports, but they're not my whole life. I mean, I swim, but I'm not as good as Pearce. I play football, but I'm not as good as Darryl."

"Don't go making these decisions too soon, Mac," warned Coach. "You've got a lot of time to think about this, and you're still growing as an athlete."

"But I don't want to be an athlete," I said. "For me it's

12

all just for fun. I don't want to work at it." Before Coach could get started on his lecture about athletics containing the best of both work and play, I said quickly, "Coach, would you write me a recommendation? I'm hoping I can get a job being a lifeguard this summer."

"Sure, Mac," he said. "But..." The first bell rang almost next to us with a sound that shook your bones. I picked up my gym bag and ran. It only hit me as I was running to class that I had put myself in a spot so that I was going to have to talk to Dad about college. It would hurt his feelings if he ran into Coach and it turned out that Coach knew more about what was on my mind than he did. How did I get myself in these fixes? I hadn't planned on talking to Dad until I had some more money in the bank.

I slid into homeroom late. Nancy Jane Patterson, who had the seat next to me, gave me a big smile. Nancy Jane has gorgeous long legs, long blond hair, and dimples. For selling toothpaste on television commercials, you could do worse than Nancy Jane. It was only her personality that was a blank. I had dated her some, but it started to kill me how she was always looking in the mirror—the rearview mirror, the living room mirror. You'd think that since *I* liked looking at Nancy Jane so much I wouldn't mind that *she* liked looking at herself, too, but it drove me crazy. Believe me, I didn't have any idea how many mirrors there were in the world until I dated Nancy Jane. I even caught her checking her reflection in a silver punch bowl once.

As we were leaving homeroom, Nancy Jane snagged me in the hall. I could tell by the light of panic in her eyes that she was about to be liberated and ask me out.

"Mac," she said, "would you like to go to the Drama

Club Awards Banquet with me?" She added hastily, "I've already got the tickets. It's two weeks from Friday."

Going to banquets is not my idea of a good time. Also, it meant putting on a suit and sitting next to Nancy Jane all night. But I've been on the asking end myself too many times to sneer in her face.

"Sounds like fun," I said, lying.

Later on, during trig, an uncomfortable thought crossed my mind. A girl who looked like Nancy Jane had plenty of guys hanging around. How come she had picked me? Could it be that she liked me? But when I gave it some thought, I decided she had picked me the way she picked a bracelet or something. She probably planned on a sort of Beauty and the Beast effect and figured that having me next to her for contrast would make her look that much better. One thing I already knew about Nancy Jane was that she never forgot her image.

That afternoon when I got home I checked out my good suit to make sure I could still get into it. Luckily, I could, because what with trying to save every penny, I had decided that if I had outgrown it I was just going to have to come down with double pneumonia the night of the awards banquet.

I called Miss Rigby and asked her to write me a recommendation, and got the address of the Silver Beach Country Club from the library. Then I wrote the letter applying for the head lifeguard job. I was so uptight about it that when I finished, the typewriter keys were sticky from sweat. It's one thing to get a job at the hometown pool where everybody knows you, and it's another to make yourself sound great on paper to people you've never met. But I had made up my mind not to make the mistake of putting off writing the letter. I really wanted that lifeguard job. I wanted it bad.

14

*   *   *

The evening of the awards banquet was pretty much what I would have predicted. You always had the feeling when you went to pick up Nancy Jane that she had hired a choreographer to chart every step she took. Nobody could ever have accused her of being spontaneous. At the banquet, she won the award for hardest-working member. I had an idea that wasn't the one she had hoped for, but it was hard to tell for sure what was going on behind that glazed smile. The low point of the evening for me was when she dumped her Waldorf salad in my lap while trying to catch a glimpse of her reflection in the windows. That meant a five-dollar cleaning bill. Not to mention how cool I felt picking mayonnaise and apples off my pants.

The next morning, Saturday, I went out to get the mail, and there—sitting on the top of the pile—was a long envelope with *Silver Beach Country Club* in metallic script at the return address corner. I ripped it open. "We regret to inform you that the position you applied for has been filled..." It figured. I walked back in the house, then unfolded the letter again and read it all the way through. They went on to say that someone else had been given the job because of his greater experience, but that I was next in line. That was no consolation. It wasn't very likely that a kid my age was going to keel over dead, and since that was the only reason I could think of for somebody giving up such a perfect job, so far as I was concerned the dream of working at Silver Beach was over.

I hadn't exactly been counting on the job. I knew all along that my chances weren't too great. So how come I felt so sick now that I knew I didn't get it? I guess deep inside me where I barely realized it, there had been some little crumbs of hope.

Mom and Dad noticed at dinner that I was feeling low. It must have been the way I wasn't eating. So I told them about my losing out on the Silver Beach job.

"But at least you have your job teaching swimming at the pool," Mom said.

I pushed a bit of shortcake across my plate and rearranged the whipped cream. "I don't think so," I said. "The pool called last week and asked if they could count on me again this year. I had to tell them I had my application in somewhere else. They said they needed to get everything settled right away and they were going to have to get somebody else."

"Oh, Mac," said Mom, helplessly.

"These things happen," said Dad. "You were right to go after the better job, and I don't see what else you could have done about the pool job here. It's just one of those things. Maybe you'll be able to find something else."

I didn't say anything. We all had a good idea of how hard it would be to get another summer job as late as April. I had intended to say something to Mom and Dad that night about my deciding against State, but there didn't seem any point in it. It would only upset them that they weren't able to send me to school where I wanted to go.

I went to my room where I could be depressed without getting on everybody's nerves. Finally, when I figured I'd get cross-eyed if I stared hopelessly at my bankbook for one more minute, I got up and bicycled over to Pearce's.

When I got there he was holed up in his room playing records. "Look what Leila sent me," he said, pulling open his sock drawer. He lifted out socks and handkerchiefs until he got to what was hidden under them—a picture of Leila about the size of a movie screen and in living color.

"Nice," I said.

"I keep it here so the family doesn't see it," he said. I could see why he did. When you saw a token of affection *that* big, it naturally occurred to you you'd better keep a close eye on Pearce or he might do something really dumb, like get married. "Leila thinks she might be able to come up to visit the first part of the summer," he said.

I was glad Pearce was happy, but his conversation had been a lot more interesting before he was in love. "That's good," I said.

Polly's voice called from outside the closed door. "Can we get started on my bookshelves now?" she asked.

"I can't now," Pearce called back. "Mac is here."

It seemed pretty unfriendly to me not to open the door to hear what Polly had to say, but that's Pearce's way. Polly went away quietly. Then a minute later she came back and called out that she was leaving a tray of cookies outside the door. Pearce opened the door to get the tray, then closed it again, as if he were holding wild beasts at bay. "You don't know how lucky you are," he said feelingly. "You have all the privacy you want at your house. People aren't always banging on your door and trying to fold your socks, dust your furniture, and give you cookies."

I thought that was pretty funny. There was Pearce with no money troubles at all, all the cookies a person could ever want to eat, and gaga in love with Leila—and he was envying me, the guy with the nowhere future and the apple salad on his pants.

"I didn't get that lifeguard job," I said.

"When did you find out?"

"Got a letter this morning."

"Rotten luck. But why is it so important to you to go someplace besides State?" he asked.

17

I had to watch my step here, because I knew Pearce was plotting to go to State in order to rendezvous with Leila, who was planning to go to the teachers' college there.

"I want to go someplace with a really good political science department," I said. "Besides, I want to break out of here and go where things are really happening."

"'Yon Cassius has a lean and hungry look,'" quoted Pearce. It's the only thing he remembers from tenth-grade English, because we had to act out the play *Julius Caesar* in class.

I squirmed. "I don't see what's so bad about having some ambition," I said.

"Nothing's wrong with it. I'm just giving you a hard time. I hope you can swing it one way or another," he said, punching me in the shoulder. "Let's go to Mamma Manelli's." Pearce has the kind of reflexes that make him a whiz at video games, and every now and then he still likes to go over to the pizza place and blow a week's allowance in quarters. "Come on," he said. "Galaga is good for your soul."

After Pearce promised Polly that he would help her build her bookcases on Sunday for sure, we finally did go to Mamma Manelli's. I have to admit that Galaga is good for Pearce's soul, at least. When those machines start making their outer space sounds and their little lights go blinking like crazy while he zaps the electronic enemies, a look of perfect peace and contentment spreads over his face. But the games don't do that much for me. And, unfortunately, I ran into Dave Taylor, who was whooping with joy that I had bowed out of my regular summer job at the pool, giving him a chance to move in. He said he hated little kids, but he had scoured the town and this was the only summer job going. Then Nancy Jane came in with another guy, but smiled at me

in a way that made me feel I was going to have to watch my step or she was going to ask me out again. And I noticed that the price of pizza had gone up fifty cents.

When I got home, Dad was in the living room with a hurt look on his face. He looked like a sad, beached whale. "I happened to run into Coach Miller just now when I went out to get milk," he said. *Oh, boy, that does it,* I thought. *The end of a perfect day.*

Chapter Three

When summer vacation started and I still hadn't dug up a summer job, I volunteered to build that brick walk Mom always wanted in the garden. Since that meant I had to dig six inches down in the clay to lay pebbles for drainage under the bricks, there was plenty of backbreaking work in the job, but there was also the satisfaction of finally laying those bricks out and tamping the sand around them. It was good to know that even if my life was a mess, when it came to bricks I was making steady progress. One afternoon when Mom got in from work, she came out to sit on the steps and watch me for a while.

"How was work?" I asked, trying to stretch out the crick in my back.

"Awful," she said. "I'm not even pretending to get anything done anymore. I just sit at the typewriter working on

my résumé. That's what everybody who's been laid off is doing. Tony Widmark got another job, but he's going to have to move to Edenton.''

At supper that night the atmosphere was fairly dismal. Dad even said, ''Maybe I should have gone in with some big firm.'' That just showed how low he was feeling, because he really loved being a DA and he'd always looked down on lawyers who did nothing but chase the almighty dollar. I guess he was thinking a few almighty dollars would come in pretty handy about now.

During dessert Dad had to get up to answer the phone. In a minute he came back to the table. ''It's for you, Mac. Earl Ellsworth.''

''I don't know any Ellsworth,'' I said, getting up. ''Do you think he's selling insurance or something?'' I headed toward the kitchen.

Mr. Ellsworth's voice had that slightly hollow sound of long distance. ''Mac Chambless?'' he said. ''This is Earl Ellsworth at Silver Beach Country Club.''

For a second my breathing seemed to stop. ''Are you there, Mac?'' he said.

''Yes, sir. I'm here.''

''We've run into some problems. Our head lifeguard had to return home today, so we're in a fix. Are you still free? Could you drive over here right away to take over for the rest of the summer? My nephew, who's the assistant lifeguard, can hold the thing together tomorrow, but he's a young kid, not at all experienced, and the sooner you can get here the better.''

''Yes sir. I can come right away.'' My breathing still hadn't gotten back to its regular rhythm, but I guess I sounded O.K. because he started going on about where I could stay and

giving me directions. I didn't understand any of it, I was so excited, but I wrote it all down.

Mom and Dad knew something good had happened when I took a flying leap over the footstool, bettering my previous record for footstool leaps by two feet.

"I wish you wouldn't do that, Mac," said Mom. "It makes the whole house shake."

"Good news?" said Dad.

"They need me for that lifeguard job at Silver Beach. Right away. Mr. Ellsworth has already lined up a cheap place for me to stay in a garage apartment near the pool. Could you drive me over tomorrow? I've got to pack!"

Mom looked a little worried. "What will you eat? I knew I should have taught you to cook. Do you know how a laundromat works? Frank, I think you'd better have a little talk with Mac."

Dad looked perfectly relaxed. "Ruth, what a DA's son doesn't know about watching out for criminals and weirdos isn't worth knowing." He pushed his chair away from the table. "Tomorrow's Saturday, right? Sure, I'll drive you over, Mac. You'd better remember to take everything you need, though, because if you forget anything we'll have to mail it to you."

It was hard to believe. It was like a dream. I was really headed toward the luscious money and the gorgeous girls of Silver Beach. My toothbrush. I'd better remember my toothbrush. "Maybe I can finish that brick walk in the fall," I said to Mom as I moved toward my room to start packing. She managed a weak smile. I thought she was worrying a lot about nothing. Laundromats must have directions put up somewhere, and a person can always eat Pepperidge Farm.

It took me quite a while to get the car packed the next morning, so we weren't able to get off until the afternoon. I could have taken the bus to Silver Beach, but I was glad Dad could drive me because that way I could strap my bike on top of the car and take it with me. It was no sports car, but it was transportation.

A couple of times on the drive over, Dad got all choked up and said they would miss me. People who have seen Dad in the courtroom, bearing down on witnesses with those bushy eyebrows of his, would be surprised to see what a softie he is as a father. I was just as glad when we finally got there. Luckily, the directions Mr. Ellsworth had given me, which seemed like so much Greek when I was writing them down, began to make sense when we got close to Silver Beach and started following them. The Beach is a long island connected to the mainland by a bridge. As we drove across the bridge, the big sea gulls perched on the bridge railings hurled insults at us in their grating voices. A few gulls were wheeling and skimming the shallow water of the intercoastal waterway, and a sailboat floated peacefully in the still water. It was like a picture. It was beautiful. And I was going to spend the rest of the summer there.

We drove off the bridge and directly into the little shopping area of the island, which is heavy on seafood restaurants and expensive dress shops but without any sign of a place you could buy something you really needed. I wondered if this place even *had* a laundromat. We turned left onto the main north-south road that runs the length of the island like the backbone of a fish. Before long we were at the address Mr. Ellsworth had given me. The street number of the place was on a post at the driveway entrance. You really couldn't see the house very well from the road on account of the tremendously

tall, thick, squared-off shrubbery around the property. I noticed they had put up a little mirror where the driveway met the road so that drivers coming through the shrubbery could inch their way out without being knocked to smithereens by oncoming traffic. If you ask me, they had carried this shrubbery thing a little too far. Once you got past the hedge, you could get a better idea of the layout of the place. The main house was a big, low-slung, old-fashioned frame house. Like a lot of houses at the beach, it faced the water, hugging the waterfront and turning its back on the road. The garage, on the other hand, was up close to the road, right against the shrubbery. It wasn't very close to the house, so you could tell it dated from the old days when grocery boys used to deliver to the house in horse and buggy, and the lady of the house didn't have to totter with all those bags from the garage to the house. You could also tell that the present owners of the house didn't use the garage, because the driveway didn't even lead there anymore. The house had a big circular drive sweeping up in front of it, and that was where they had their cars parked. The house was nice, but the garage was just a garage.

We walked up the unpainted wooden stairs to the front door of the little apartment and found the key was under the mat just where Mr. Ellsworth had said it would be. It was pretty clear to me that Mr. Ellsworth hadn't grown up in a DA's household, or he would never had done something so dumb as leaving the key under the mat. When we stepped inside, Dad looked at the bare bulb hanging in the middle of the bedroom/living room and said, "I can see why it's cheap."

I put my duffel bag on the bed. "It's especially cheap," I said, "because the people in the big house go away during

25

the summer sometimes and like to have somebody living in the apartment to keep an eye on the house. Mr. Ellsworth explained all that to me when he called. Boy, am I lucky to have this place!'' There was a rug made of sewed-together carpet samples in the middle of the floor. In front of the bare bed, which doubled as a sofa, there was a little coffee table with a top of unpainted plywood and shapely brown glass legs, which I finally recognized as empty bottles. "Cle-ver!'' I exclaimed. "I wonder how they got the bottles to stick to the plywood?''

Dad walked into the tiny kitchen off the main room. "Well, at least you've got a nice view,'' he said. "If you stand at the kitchen sink, you can see the water. Good for when you're doing dishes.''

I didn't say so, but I didn't plan to be washing many dishes. Paper plates and TV dinners would see me through. As he walked back into the room, I sat down on the bed and gave a couple of bounces. I could hear the *boing* of a spring breathing its last. "This is really going to be great,'' I said. "What a bargain.''

"I'm glad we haven't brought you up to be a slave to the creature comforts,'' Dad said, "but I'm also glad your mother isn't here to see this place.''

I could see what he meant. The place wasn't Mom's cup of tea, but then she wasn't going to be living there.

Dad looked at the bare mattress on the bed with sudden misgiving. "Did you remember to bring sheets?'' he said.

"Yep,'' I said proudly. "They're in the trunk.''

"Well, you're on your own now,'' Dad said. "But I want you to call your mother and me collect every weekend to keep us posted on how you're getting along. And you be sure to take good care of yourself.''

"I will. Don't worry about me.''

"I'm not worried," said Dad in a hearty voice. "I know you'll get along fine. I trust you completely."

Dad and Mom say different things, but actually they worry about exactly the same things. So I laid it on thick about how I would eat plenty of green vegetables and not speak to criminals and weirdos, and finally he was able to bring himself to help me finish unloading the car and shove off for home.

After he left, it was so quiet in the apartment it was actually kind of spooky. I went into the kitchen and stood looking out at the water. Lights were starting to come on in the village across the waterway, and a flock of birds was coming in toward the island to roost, hundreds of tiny black silhouettes. Then I saw that the lights in the main house were coming on, which made the place seem a bit more cozy. *I'm really on my own now,* I thought. I figured I was going to like it.

It took me quite a while to get the place cleaned up and squared away, but luckily I was able to sleep late the next morning because the pool didn't open until one on Sunday. I went in a little early to introduce myself and look the place over. I found Mr. Ellsworth with no trouble, but he was up to his ears with getting the Sunday buffet lunch under way. Families were already starting to get there, so he just shook my hand, pointed me toward the pool, and wished me luck. It was great that he had all this confidence in me, I thought, but it would have been more of a help if he had been able to show me where the utility shed was; where they kept the chlorine and skimming nets; where the telephone, the soft drink machine, the locker room, and other things were.

When I got outside I still didn't see where the locker room

was, but luckily I was wearing my swim trunks under my jeans, so I just shucked the jeans in a little alley that ran between the golf pro's shop and the main building. While I was standing with one foot in my jeans and one foot out, I was almost run down by a golf cart tearing down the alley. I made a mental note that the alley led to the golf cart park. I could tell life was going to be full of unpleasant surprises until I found my way around.

Kids were already milling around at the gate to the pool. At the stroke of one I unlocked the gate with the key Mr. Ellsworth had given me and opened the pool. I climbed up to the lifeguard's seat under the big umbrella and tried to look like a head lifeguard. Kids started streaming in, also mothers carrying strollers and playpens. It was amazing how fast the place filled up. I began to feel a little panicky. Why did everybody have to come exactly at one o'clock? Didn't these people ever hear about taking your time over your Sunday lunch? Didn't any of them ever think of playing tennis instead? Did every living soul on the island have to stream into my pool? I had filled in at the city pool at home now and then, but there had always been other lifeguards around, too. I had never covered the whole pool alone. Come to think of it, where was that assistant lifeguard Mr. Ellsworth had told me about?

All the awful pool accidents I had ever heard about began to flood my mind. I wished I had my Red Cross first-aid book with me just to skim over a bit and refresh my memory, but I knew that even if I had it, I wouldn't have been able to take my eyes off the pool for a minute for fear something awful would happen.

At about twenty after one, a cave-chested kid climbed up in the other lifeguard's chair at the shallow end of the pool. The

assistant guy was here at last. But one-twenty was a funny time to be coming in to work. I was sure he should have been there at one, like me. I decided I had better be firm about that from the beginning. After all, even though the idea was going to take some getting used to, I was in charge.

I climbed down from my chair and walked around to introduce myself. He was a sort of limp-looking guy. A hank of straight brown hair hung in his face, his nose was covered with zinc oxide, and his shoulders were peeling. He muttered that his name was Brandon. For all I knew, old Brandon was the best lifeguard in three counties, but one thing was for sure—he didn't get the job for his personality.

"I'm really glad to see you," I said. "But make sure you get here at one next time. This place fills up fast."

Personality Boy didn't say anything. I made my way back to my chair. This was going to be sticky. I recalled that Brandon was Mr. Ellsworth's nephew. I was going to have to be diplomatic but firm. If that didn't work, it might be a long summer. After I got back on my perch, adjusted my sunglasses, and started scanning the pool again for possible disasters, it hit me that maybe Brandon had wanted my job. Maybe when the regular lifeguard had to leave all of a sudden, he figured his moment of glory had come. If that was what was going on, it would explain why he was being such a pain. It was awkward, though. I sure didn't feel like asking him to show me around.

Over near the slide, I saw a kid holding another kid's head under water, so I let go with my whistle. He jumped back guiltily, and the other kid—no fool—swam away fast. "Cut that out!" I yelled. "Any more of that, and it's out of the pool for ten minutes."

I swept an eye over Brandon's half of the pool. I'd have felt better if it looked like Brandon had the sense God gave a gnat. In some ways his end of the pool was easier, because at the shallow end the parents were always right there with the kids and usually kept a pretty close eye on them. In another way, though, it was harder, because you were dealing with a heck of a lot of little nonswimmers, and it didn't take long for them to go under and get full of water, particularly if a couple of the parents started talking to each other instead of watching the kids. I surveyed that end of the pool anxiously. I noticed one mother who had three little kids, but she seemed to have them pretty much under control. She was standing in the water, and the kids were taking turns jumping off the pool's edge and into her arms. There was a whole horde of kids about six or seven years old who could swim some and whose mothers were sitting in deck chairs writing letters. At the far end there was a young blond girl with a little redheaded kid. All of a sudden I realized that the young blond was Polly Barron! I remembered then that she had gotten a summer job being a mother's helper somewhere. I guessed that after my lifeguard job hadn't panned out, Pearce hadn't wanted to mention that Polly was getting to go to Silver Beach.

I glanced at the big clock and saw that it was almost two o'clock. I blew my whistle. "Break!" I yelled. "Everybody out." Brandon's whistle echoed mine. "Break! Break!" Kids started crawling out of the pool. Then began the golden ten minutes out of every hour when the lifeguards were entitled to swill sodas, stretch their legs, and blink their weary eyes. I made a beeline for Polly. A wave of relief swept over me. I knew Polly had been there for weeks. She'd be able to show me the ropes. And something I hadn't realized until I saw her

30

was that I was just a little bit lonely. What a break that she was here!

She smiled when I walked up to her. "Mac! So you're the new lifeguard!" she said. She turned to the little redheaded kid. "Brian, this is my friend Mac." Brian narrowed his eyes, then hauled off and landed me one right in the stomach. *"Ooof,"* I said. He looked about five, but he had a pretty respectable punch. He laughed with delight. "Brian, we do not hit people in the stomach," said Polly firmly, removing him beyond hitting range. I didn't really care if the kid hit me in the stomach because my stomach is in pretty good shape, but I could see it wasn't something you wanted to encourage in a kid with that strong a right arm.

"Hey, am I glad to see you!" I said. "You've got to tell me where everything is. There don't seem to be any signs up anywhere, and Ellsworth didn't tell me a thing. Where the heck is the locker room?"

Polly's eyes crinkled into a smile. The short wisps of hair around her face were dry, but the rest of her hair was hanging down wet in the uneven way hair does when you get out of the pool. She reminded me of that famous picture I always think of as "Venus on the Half-Shell," except that Venus didn't have a dusting of freckles across her nose the way Polly does. She pointed out the inconspicuous locker rooms, the concealed soft drink machine, and the hidden telephone. Honestly, you'd think the club was set up to stop a foreign invasion the way they had everything hidden away.

"I wanna get back in the pool," complained Brian. "When is break gonna be over, Polly?"

"It's just started," said Polly reasonably. "Let me put

31

some more suntan lotion on you, and you'll be all ready to go in when Mac blows the whistle." —

"Don't want to put on suntan lotion," said Brian.

"Now you don't want to end up looking like Brandon, do you?" Polly said. Brian took a look at Brandon skulking off toward the drink machine with his zinc oxide nose and peeling shoulders and decided to let Polly put on the suntan lotion after all.

"Look at those guys," Brian said. "They're getting in the pool."

"Out of the pool, kids!" I yelled. "Break isn't over."

The six-year-olds climbed out and sat dangling their feet over the edge, looking at me sideways and calculating their chances of getting creamed if they slipped in again. A girl about my age called Polly. It turned out to be Lindsay, Polly's neighbor. She had blond hair twisted up in a barrette and was wearing a hot-pink swimsuit that didn't leave much to the imagination. She was a pretty girl and friendly, but not really my type. I can admire what it takes to get a gorgeous deep tan like that with no splotches or strap marks and all oiled and gleaming in the sun, but I always figure any girl who would waste so much effort getting baked in the sun that way has got to be a little bit nuts. Still, she seemed to be a nice girl, and she asked Polly to bring me along to a party she was having over the weekend. Things were looking up for me at Silver Beach.

I blew the whistle to end the break, and all the kids plunged in, sounding like a pack of hyenas ready to do their worst. By then I was feeling a lot better. So far nobody had killed themselves, I was beginning to find my way around, and Polly was there. A little twelve-year-old with a bathing suit so skimpy it hardly counted and a figure ditto hung on

my chair and looked up at me worshipfully. She had strap marks all over the place and a peeling nose. "Are you the new lifeguard?" she breathed. "What's your name?"

I grinned. The summer had really begun. She was my first groupie.

Chapter Four

One thing I hadn't realized about the job of head lifeguard was that it also meant I was in charge of the swimming team. But I've been on swim teams all my life, so I didn't figure it would be any problem. Since Monday was the day the pool was chlorinated and time-off for lifeguards, the first day of swimming practice was Tuesday. At four o'clock I blew the whistle and cleared the pool of all the mamas and babies and all the six-year-olds who thought they were kamikaze pilots— time for civilians to clear out and for swim practice to begin. Then the swim team, all of them in matching green swim-suits, swarmed in. If you're a lifeguard, you kind of get in the habit of recognizing people by their suits, and when all these kids appeared in identical swimsuits, I swear I couldn't tell one from another. What I had on my hands was mass confusion. There were splashes here and there as kids jumped

in the pool or got thrown in, and there was lots of giggling and screaming. I wished they had their names tattooed on their foreheads. With such a solid bunch of bodies, "Hey you!" wasn't much good. I noticed that Brandon, sitting on the pool's edge, looked cheerful, a bad sign. It was up to me to bring order into this mess. "All right!" I yelled. "Let's everybody get into age groups. All the nines and older line up by Brandon, sixes and below line up over here, and sevens and eights in between." The confusion picked up some as some kids tried to get into line and others tried to get into some last-minute trouble. I grabbed a couple of kids as they went by. "Hey, you," I said, "get over there by Brandon. You're seven, aren't you? And you, don't you move. You stay here with me." It was like rounding up dogies on a cattle drive, but finally three lines appeared. "Brandon!" I yelled. "You take the nines and ups to the deep end and start 'em swimming laps. All the rest of you kids line up here at the edge of the pool. When I give the word, you kids kick off and swim straight to the other side as fast as you can."

At the signal they all jumped in and started swimming, but I wouldn't say they went fast. They didn't exactly go straight, either. In fact, they more or less wallowed all over the place. I tried to remember if I had foundered around like that when I was little. "Don't wiggle!" I yelled. "Keep those bodies straight! Keep your eyes on the lines on the bottom of the pool! Straight, Straight!"

They didn't look to me like the next generation of Olympic champs, but I had to be careful not to discourage them. Nobody ever built up a team by telling everybody how awful they were. When they'd all got to the other side of the pool, I

tried to be optimistic. "A good start," I said. "Now let's take a look at those kicks, everybody. Watch me."

I was really glad when swim practice was finally over and the mamas started driving up in the parking lot. It wasn't just that I was bushed. I needed to go by the store and pick up something for dinner. I also needed to wash my socks. One thing I had noticed about living away from home was how much time it took just to keep yourself fed and make sure you had enough clean socks. Looking back on my life at home, it seemed like I'd been living in a luxury hotel with room service.

But even if I did have to wash my own socks, I knew I was going to have fun at Silver Beach. One good thing I'd already found out was that there was a paved bike trail all along the intercoastal waterway side of the island, the side where there weren't any breakers—just still water, sea gulls, and fishermen. I could bike almost the whole way from the pool to my apartment using that bike trail. Along the way I would pass other people bicycling, sometimes whole families. People did a lot of bicycling at Silver Beach. It was one place in the world where it was almost better to have a bike than a sports car.

Every now and then I had to work the after-supper shift. The crowd was light then and one guard could cover it. Brandon and I and the other lifeguard, a good kid named Maggie, took turns doing it, so each of us only had to do it twice a week. I was sure glad not to be stuck with it every night, because a lot of times there was something going on I didn't want to miss, particularly on the weekend. Silver Beach was one long round of parties of one kind and another.

My first party was the beach bash given by Lindsay. Luckily, I didn't have to work that night, because I was really

looking forward to it. I had had all week to look over the girls at the pool, but although everybody was friendly, there hadn't been time to really get to know anybody while I was trying to keep an eye on a hundred kids.

I was a little bit late going to pick Polly up for the party because it took me a little while to find the right house. The family she was working for, the MacDougals, had rented a place on the surf side just a few blocks from the club pool. I parked my bike there, and Polly and I walked down to the beach together. It wasn't dark yet, but you could see the bonfire on the beach marking the place of the party. It looked like some kids were playing ball, and even from a distance you could hear shrieks and laughing. Polly seemed really happy. "Don't you think Lindsay is nice, Mac? I like everybody here. I just love it all."

When we got there Polly was swept up right away by her friends. She sure was at home. Lindsay came over to say hi. She was wearing some sort of sarong thing over her swimsuit and, as usual, looked gleaming brown. "There's the cooler," she said, flashing me a smile showing very white teeth. "The potato chips and the hot dogs are on the table."

"Hey, Mac!" somebody yelled. "We need another man for volleyball. Harry and Dave are flaking out on us."

I could see I had a problem. Everybody knew my name. After all, I was pretty conspicuous sitting up in my lifeguard's chair at the pool all week. But I wasn't too sure of anybody else's. There was a broad stretch of beach because the tide was going down, but there was no shortage of kids, either, and the place looked crowded and confusing. At least some of the faces looked familiar from my having seen them at the pool. When volleyball wound down, I found myself a cold

drink and tried to tell myself that it wasn't going to be too hard to tack names and personalities onto those faces.

Polly appeared at my side, her cheeks flushed. "Have you been meeting people, Mac?" she said. "Come on, and I'll introduce you to some of my friends." Well, here was a chance to get some names, so I padded along after her, squishing sand between my toes.

"Mona," said Polly to a girl with hip-length black hair, "this is a friend of mine from home, Mac Chambless."

"You're the new lifeguard," Mona said. I admitted it.

"And this is Skip Harris, Allen Winkle, and Art Fulford," said Polly. I noticed that among Polly's friends the boys outnumbered the girls three to two.

"Have you cooked your hot dog yet?" said Winkle. "Why don't you come sit with us when you do?"

The sun was going down and the breeze was coming off the ocean. Time to start moving toward the fire to cook a hot dog. The trick with cooking hot dogs over a bonfire, I always figure, is to cook the hot dog and not yourself. An unbent coat hanger doesn't give you a whole lot of distance from the flames, and by the time my hot dog started to look all black and blistered the way it should, my face was beginning to feel fairly roasted, too. I like my hot dogs with everything on them, and I mean everything—chili, chopped onions, coleslaw. I piled it high. Mona, who was standing next to me, looked at my dinner and shuddered.

I settled down with Polly's friends in a semicircle not far from the bonfire, but upwind from the blowing cinders. "That's really something, that you and Polly know each other," said Winkle. "Nobody's ever here from my hometown."

I opened my mouth to tell him how I used to give Polly piggyback rides, but as if she could read my mind, Polly

39

jumped in and started talking about the MacDougal kids. I was glad, because when I thought about it, I didn't want to say anything that might make Polly feel like a baby around her friends. When you're around a bunch of strangers, you're so hard up for something to say you sometimes say something you wish you hadn't.

"Mrs. MacDougal," Polly was saying, "told my mother she figured she was doing a public service by getting girls to baby-sit for her. She says a few hours with Brian, Mark, and Tracy will convince anybody not to get married too early."

"Has it convinced you?" leered Winkle, grabbing Polly's big toe.

Polly laughed. "I'm not getting married young," she said. "No danger. I want to see the world." She wiggled her toes in the sand.

Personally, I thought the way that guy Winkle hung on Polly was pretty disgusting. He kept looking into her eyes, if you know what I mean.

"Why don't we go see if we can find a sea turtle?" said Lindsay, after we'd cleared our plates.

"Sea turtle?" I said.

"This is their egg-laying season," explained Lindsay. "They're a protected species, and the fish and game commission patrols this whole shore, but there's no law against looking at the turtles. And once they start laying, nothing you do bothers them. You can sit right down on them, and they don't pay a bit of attention."

To me, that didn't sound very polite to the turtle, but I supposed it was harmless enough. Lindsay stood up and yelled, "Who wants to go turtle-watching?" Except for the kids playing tag on the dunes, everybody started walking down the beach. I walked next to Polly in case old Winkle

40

should decide to make himself obnoxious again. It was amazing, I thought, how people grew up before you knew it. Of course, I had noticed before that Polly was getting older, but somehow it hadn't really hit me that she was almost grown up. That night she was wearing a sweatshirt and short cut-offs, so you could see what nice legs she had. I've always had a weakness for good legs. And her hair had a nice, fresh, clean smell as if she washed it a lot. All in all, I guessed it wasn't too surprising that Winkle hung around. I would have to keep an eye on him. Polly might be a big girl now, but she hadn't been around much.

"Look, everybody!" yelled Lindsay. "Tracks."

Ahead of us it looked as if a tractor had driven up out of the ocean. Deep furrows had been cut in the sand by the flippers of a huge turtle. Everybody got quiet, and we followed the tracks up the shore, where they made a U-turn and went out to the ocean again.

"She changed her mind," said Lindsay in disappointment.

No wonder, in my opinion. All those kids whooping and hollering probably convinced the sea turtle she'd better find a quieter neighborhood for her babies. I looked out to sea. The moonlight skimmed across the ocean. Somewhere out there was swimming a gigantic sea turtle waiting for us all to go home. *Good luck, sea turtle,* I thought.

We turned around and headed back to the fire. We had ended up walking quite a distance. After we got back, Polly said, "I'd better be getting home. Mrs. MacDougal wouldn't care if I stayed out a little later, but the twins get up pretty early, and by this time of night I get sleepy."

"I'll walk you home," I said.

"Oh, you don't have to do that," said Polly. "I can see the house from here. It's no distance at all."

"I know I don't have to," I said. "I want to."

Winkle came running over. "Going home, Polly?" he said.

"She's tired," I said firmly. "I'm walking her home."

Winkle looked a little taken aback. "O.K. Well, nice meeting you, Mac. See you tomorrow, Polly."

We walked up the path between the dunes, crossing the narrow paved path along the dunes that the fish and game commission uses for patroling. The sounds of the party got a bit dimmer as we moved toward the MacDougals' house.

"What did Winkle mean when he said he was going to see you tomorrow?" I said. Once I said this, I was embarrassed to realize that it was a very nosy question, but Polly didn't seem to mind. "Oh, Allen works at the snack bar at the club," she said. "That's a regular stop for me when I've got Brian or the twins. They're crazy about the snack shop." It occurred to me I had better check out the snack shop. I was getting pretty tired of the oatmeal cookies and potato chips out of the vending machine, anyway.

We walked along for a while without saying anything. I thought about how blonds like Polly look good in the moonlight. Moonlight seems to lie on their hair and pick out silver strands of it.

"You know back at the party when you said you wanted to see the world?" I said finally. "What sort of thing do you have in mind?"

"Travel," Polly said promptly. "I'd like to see New York, for instance."

"Hmmm," I said noncommittally. I had seen New York City and once was enough—all that soot in the air and little

old ladies wandering around with all their belongings in shopping bags. But I admired Polly's sense of adventure.

"My real goal is to be able to get a job as a nanny in some country like Italy or France," Polly went on enthusiastically. "Really *live* in another country. That's why this job with Mrs. MacDougal is such a good thing for me. It's experience. Later on, maybe I can use the reference."

I was amazed that all those wild yearnings had come boiling out from sweet little Polly, although I don't know why it should have surprised me. I had a lot of wild ideas and dreams that people didn't suspect, too.

"Of course, all of this is a long way off," Polly added.

"Sure," I said. I hesitated a minute and then plunged in. "You know, I want to see the world, too. What I want is to be where things really happen—D.C. Maybe be a congressman's aide. Learn the ins and outs of politics. Someday maybe run for office."

Polly looked interested.

"I don't want to spend my whole life in Fairview," I said. "I want to make something of myself."

I had never told anybody so much about my dreams, and I felt embarrassed, but Polly was an easy girl to talk to. Later on I realized that the night of Lindsay's beach party was a kind of turning point in the summer. That was when I quit thinking of Polly as a kid and started thinking of her as a girl.

She looked at me with those clear blue eyes of hers and didn't say anything. I began to feel a little funny that I had gotten so wound up talking about my future. It wasn't like me.

"I think I know what you mean," said Polly finally. "Fairview is a great place to live when you're little, but when you start to grow up you get to feeling you need more room.

It kind of limits you to be surrounded by people who knew you when you were five."

That was exactly the way I felt about it, but I had an unpleasant thought. It hit me suddenly that I had known Polly since she was five. I hope she wasn't feeling that I was one of those people she'd like to get away from.

She picked up a pebble and tossed it ahead of us on the street. It was a shiny white pebble and seemed to dance for a minute in the moonlight as it bounced. "Of course, later," she said, "I may move back to Fairview and start putting things in my attic."

"Putting things in your attic?"

"Once people start stacking stuff up in their attic, they never go anywhere. It's like a natural law. They're glued to their stuff."

"Scrapbooks and things."

"And broken lamps and old beds and Halloween costumes. You should see my grandmother's attic. People get tied down other ways, too. Like my mother has her garden. She can't stand to go away and let the weeds get ahead of her. And my Uncle Ralph won't go anyplace, either. He says he's comfortable at home and can't see trotting off to other countries where his stomach would get upset. He says he stayed in a motel in Raleigh once and the beds were no good." Polly considered her unadventurous family a moment in melancholy silence, then said, "I want to get my traveling done before that happens to me."

By then we were back at the MacDougals' house. Mrs. M. came to the door to let Polly in, and Polly introduced me. Mrs. M. looked me over carefully, then smiled and shook my hand. I guess she felt she had to look after Polly.

I got on my bike and headed home. It was weird to be

riding along the streets at eleven o'clock, but nice. You can smell a lot more at night, and Silver Beach has a nice, salty, ocean smell. I hit the bike trail and was soon riding soundlessly along beside the still waterway, watching the moon reflected in the water and soaking in the nice summery feel of the island. I really liked Silver Beach. I realized that I liked it even better because Polly was there.

Chapter Five

Another week of slaving at the pool and I was ready for another party. Luckily, Mona had her pig-pickin' on Friday night instead of Saturday, when the team had a swim meet. I went by to get Polly, because she knew where Mona's place was. Actually, that wasn't the only reason I went by to pick up Polly. I thought it would be nice to have a little quiet time to talk to her before we hit all the commotion at the party. I biked over to the MacDougals', and we walked to Mona's together.

The van from Friendly's Barbecue was at the party with one of those enormous metal ovens that look like fat torpedoes on wheels, the thing the pig gets barbecued in. Friendly's had put the trailer oven in the backyard next to some long tables loaded down with food. The oven was open, and a whiff of roasted pork blew in our direction. Personally, I'm

not absolutely crazy about the food that gets served at a pig-pickin', but one thing you can say about it, I've never heard anybody claim there wasn't enough. There were great heaps of food wherever you looked. A man in a battered white hat was standing at the long table serving rolls, succotash, and deep-fried cornbread, which is more like a cornbread potato chip than anything else. "You guys got here just in time," Winkle called to us as we came up. "I'm so hungry I'm about to eat all this stuff up." The man in the white hat cracked a sour smile and added two more soft rolls to Winkle's plate. Mona waved at us and came over, her black hair swinging. "I'm so glad you could make it, Mac," she said. "I was afraid you'd have to work tonight. We had to schedule the caterer weeks ago, so there was no switching it."

"Brandon's got duty tonight," I said.

Mona made sympathetic sounds. I thought it showed an extra kind heart on her part to sympathize with Brandon, but then maybe other people took to him more than I did.

The evening air was as warm as a bath. Over on the deck you could see a jukebox glowing. It was playing so loud you could even hear it above the noise of the crowd. Kids were milling about everywhere. "Save the first dance for me," Art said to Polly as he passed us, balancing his plate on one hand. We got in line, got our plates filled by the man in the white hat, then moved on to the pig. It was stretched out on the spit, all one hundred pounds of it, its skin turned to crackling and an apple in its mouth. Now came the tricky part. You could cut your pork off anyplace you wanted, but you needed to know something about what pork looks like before it's done up in cellophane if you wanted to get the part you

48

planned on. Luckily, practice had made me pretty good at finding the loin.

Mona's cousin Ellen, who was visiting for the week, was behind us in line. You could recognize her right away, because her legs were so white they sort of glowed in the dark.

"*Ugh,*" she said. "I can't look at the thing. Polly, will you cut me a piece so I can just go by it with my eyes closed?"

"Sure," said Polly. "What piece do you want?"

"Does the thing have pork chops?" said Ellen.

"Of course it had pork chops," grinned Polly. "It's a pig." She sliced a hunk out of the loin and put it on Ellen's plate. Ellen opened her eyes and looked at the rough chunk on her plate. "It doesn't look like a pork chop," she said uncertainly.

"It's the same thing, though," Polly assured her.

Ellen was from Cincinnati, and she was obviously suffering from culture shock at her first pig-pickin'.

"Why don't you sit with us?" I said to Ellen, trying to make her feel more at home. She looked a little happier.

"Look," said Polly, "there are some places over there where Allen is." Winkle saw us eyeing his table and gave us a friendly wave. It looked like there was no help for it. Ellen and I followed Polly over to Winkle's table. It struck me that it would be nice if Ellen and Winkle turned out to be soulmates and went dancing off into the sunset together. I wasn't too crazy about the way Winkle and Polly were always talking together.

Mona stopped by at our table. "You didn't get any Sally Lunn bread!" she said. "Let me get you some. It's the one thing I made myself." Pretty soon, Mona came back with a plate of her bread. It was good, too.

Later on, when people finished eating, they started dancing on the deck to the jukebox. Bobby Sherridan climbed up on the deck railing and called out that he was going to fly, but then Mona's dad appeared like a dark shadow at the back door, and Bobby climbed down quickly with an awkward cough.

"Everybody having a good time, Mona?" her dad rumbled.

"Yes, Daddy," she said.

"Well, you kids see to it that you don't have *too* good a time," he said.

"Yes, sir!" we all echoed.

We danced some more after that, but finally Polly started yawning and she and I decided to move on home. The party was still going strong when we left, fueled by kids who didn't have to get up early in the morning. Polly had worn a swirly sort of sundress with straps that weren't worth mentioning and little pink ballet slippers. As we walked back, she paused a moment and, balancing on one foot, pulled off a shoe and held it up to the moon. "It looks like I danced a hole in my shoe," she said. "I can see the moon through the sole."

"If that's the worst trouble you have, you're in good shape," I said. "Now me, I have real troubles. The swim team has a meet tomorrow."

"You'll survive," said Polly, smiling at me.

But the next afternoon when I faced the swim meet, I wasn't so sure Polly was right. I was so uptight about it you'd think it was some championship match and that I was swimming. We were up against the Willow Green Athletic Club, which was mostly made up of kids from the town of Silver Glen, just across from us, on the mainland. They had a strong team and had won the meet the year before, so you'd think

everybody would have been rooting for us—the underdogs. They weren't, though. The people whose kids didn't swim on either team were rooting mostly for Willow Green. I think the reason for this was that we were a country club team. There's a lot of prejudice against country clubs. I can understand that. Sometimes I feel prejudiced against country clubs myself. It's just that this summer the country club team happened to be *my* team.

I was pretty nervous about the match. I had been drilling the kids for weeks, but now it was all up to them. I just hoped nobody sank or threw up. Parents were starting to find seats in the temporary bleachers, and the ribbons were all laid out in neat order at the judges' table. I signaled Brandon to get the older kids together. I had ended up letting him take the older kids because it was a cinch he didn't have the right touch with the little kids. Actually, I wished I had been able to have Maggie help me with the team instead, but Brandon seemed to have seniority or something. He had been helping the other lifeguard before I came, and I didn't think it would be smart to produce more bad feeling by bumping him. I called the little kids together and got in a huddle with them for a pep talk. It was my first pep talk, and it wasn't exactly a masterpiece.

"I know you can do it," I said, "and if you do your very, very best, I won't be ashamed of you no matter what happens." At least the second part of that was true, but I was afraid it didn't hit quite the right optimistic note.

"I feel sick to my stomach," said Christy, looking a bit green.

"Yuck. She's going to throw up," said Stephen, rolling his eyes in disgust.

"Take some deep breaths, Christy," I said, "and think of

51

something nice." I took a few deep breaths myself to show her how it was done. The something nice I thought of was the match being over. "Just remember everything I told you and slip off that starting block fast like a frog," I said. "Now Christy, Stephen, and Jeff—you're first. Go get in your starting places. We're going to be right here cheering you, aren't we team?"

Christy tottered over to her starting block. I sure hoped she wasn't going to throw up. Should I pull her? No, I decided to take my chances. If she did O.K., it would give her confidence, but if I pulled her now, she'd be even more nervous at the next meet. I noticed that the three kids on the other side, the Willow Green kids, seemed to be real cool. I wished I was as cool as they looked.

At the bang of the starting gun, all the kids hit the water. In Jeff's case he literally hit the water. I winced as I heard the smack of the belly whopper. "Go kids! Go!" I yelled. Beside me all those little piping voices yelled, "Go!" I could hear hysterical shrieks from the parents in the stands. Christy won the heat, but I didn't have time to enjoy it. In minutes I had other worries. I was lining up three kids for the next heat.

By the time the match was over, I was more or less numb, but to my surprise we had copped a total of five blue ribbons. Christy nearly passed out when she got hers. The parents came streaming down from the stands, and I started gathering my stuff together to bike home. Just then a kid tapped me on the shoulder and said, "They want to see you over at the judges' table."

Clear as my conscience was, that did give me a little jolt. I walked over to the judges' table. There were no ribbons on it but it was still stacked with papers, and sitting around it were some upset-looking judges. "Mac," Mr. Brown said, his

brow creased, "Coach Thomas from Willow Green has just lodged a complaint. He says he has reason to believe that one of the kids in your six-and-below class is really seven."

I could feel the blood drain down to my toes. "Who?" I croaked.

Mr. Evans looked at a piece of paper he was holding. "Tommy Brisbane, he says."

"Oh no!" I said. I realized I couldn't swear Tommy was six. I hadn't seen anybody's birth certificate. I got an awful, sick feeling as I remembered the first day of practice when I had sorted them all out into age groups. Could it be that Tommy had been so shy he didn't want to tell me he was in the wrong group? Or so unsure of himself that he actually wanted to swim with the younger group? I steadied myself against the judges' table with one hand.

"Of course, we have to look into this," said Mr. Evans. "But what we're planning to do is this: We're going to set up a meeting tomorrow between the coaches of both teams at Earl Ellsworth's office and let all of you work it out. I hope we can transfer the ribbon to the rightful winner with a minimum of fuss and publicity. I don't like to see a child as young as Tommy involved in something like this. I'm going to hold off reporting the winners to the paper until we get this matter settled."

It was a miracle I got home on my bike without getting run down by a car. My mind was churning like a blender. I wondered how Coach Green knew Tommy was seven. I was pretty sure he wouldn't have brought the complaint unless he was on solid ground. Probably some kid on the Willow Green team was in Tommy's class at school. For a second I played with the idea that maybe Tommy was a grade ahead in school—that it was all a mix-up and that it was going to turn

out O.K.—but when I examined that idea closely, it looked pretty feeble. If there was one thing kids knew about other kids, it was how old they were. Since being older was such a status thing among kids, everybody in the class would know who was already seven and who wasn't. It looked to me like a pretty sure thing that Tommy was seven.

I parked my bike under my stairs, locked it, and dragged myself up to my apartment. Of course, this probably meant goodbye summer job. Once Mr. Ellsworth established that I had brought shame to the name of Silver Beach Country Club, he was going to show me the door pretty quick. But my mind didn't stop there. I was already imagining myself in years to come campaigning to be the next senator from North Carolina when suddenly someone would dig up "that sordid affair" at the Silver Beach Country Club. It would be hard for a young senator to look honest with that sort of cloud hanging over him. And the fear that somebody was going to dig it up would keep me on pins and needles my entire life.

How could I have been so dumb, so careless? I threw myself on the bed with a groan. Later on, after I had pulled myself together into a kind of calm depression, I called Dad and told him the whole story.

"Do you want me to drive over?" he said.

"I don't know," I said. "On the one hand I'd kind of like to have my lawyer present, but on the other hand I feel like I'm too old to have my father show up."

"I've got a trial on my hands here, anyway," said Dad, "and I think it's a little premature to be talking about lawyers. Call me tomorrow and let me know how that meeting at Ellsworth's office goes. It's quite possible that everyone will see you made an honest mistake, and it will go no further."

"I hope so," I said, but when I pictured the round, red face of the Willow Green coach, I knew that it was definitely the face of a man out for blood. I spent a very miserable night creasing the sheets as I tossed and turned.

The next afternoon, I put on the most respectable clothes I had brought with me and bicycled to the club for the meeting. As I went in the club building, I could see Brandon and Maggie in the distance sitting in the lifeguards' chairs at the pool. They looked so carefree I wished I could have changed places.

Mr. Ellsworth's office was heavy on mahogany, deep carpets, and draperies. It looked expensive. It occurred to me that maybe this wasn't the best place to encourage a spirit of cooperation in the underpaid Willow Green coaches. "The Willow Green coaches ought to be here any minute," said Mr. Ellsworth. "Did you know that Tommy was seven?" he added, coming straight to the point.

"No, sir," I said. "Are you sure he is?"

"I talked to his parents last night. Of course, they're terribly upset, a kid Tommy's age being involved in something like this. They aren't swimmers themselves, and it appears they didn't even realize the kids were divided into age groups. They said Tommy will return the blue ribbon, but they want him kept completely out of it." He paused a minute. "Uh, their lawyer called me this morning," he added.

I took this to mean that Tommy most certainly was going to be kept out of it.

The door opened, and the Willow Green coach and his two assistants came in.

"Come right in, gentlemen," said Mr. Ellsworth jovially. The Willow Green coach had the expression of a stone

statue—but mad. I didn't find it reassuring. "Have a seat," urged Mr. Ellsworth. "Now, Mac, why don't you tell everyone just what happened."

"I'm not sure exactly what happened," I said. "I just got here a couple of weeks ago, and I didn't know any of the kids. The first day I sorted them out into age groups. Later, a couple of kids told me they were in the wrong group, and I switched them. I figured all of them would make sure they were in the right group. I mean, I had no idea anybody was out of their own group. The only thing I can think of is that Tommy was just too shy to speak to me. I just don't understand it."

"You see," Mr. Ellsworth explained, "we had to call Mac in at the last minute when our regular lifeguard had a family emergency. Mac's not from around here, and he hadn't had time to get to know the kids. It was just an unfortunate mistake."

The Willow Green coach looked skeptical. The two assistant coaches had their hands folded over their chests. Taking a look at those three, my words would have stuck in my throat, but Mr. Ellsworth seemed unshaken.

"Of course, we'll return the blue ribbon," he said. "I don't believe that anyone intended this to happen, and I just hope we can handle this with no publicity."

The Willow Green coach narrowed his eyes. "When do we get the ribbon?"

Mr. Ellsworth produced it from his top desk drawer. "I happen to have it right here," he said. "And Ed Brown has already changed the official record accordingly."

The Willow Green coach did not smile.

"Uh, perhaps you would like him to give you a call confirming that," said Mr. Ellsworth.

"Yep," said the Willow Green coach.

Mr. Ellsworth took a deep breath. "Well, I want to thank you for your understanding in this very painful matter," he said. "Thank you for coming."

The Willow Green staff departed, darting suspicious glances behind them as they left. Mr. Ellsworth closed the door behind them with obvious relief. He walked over to a cabinet near the window and poured himself a drink. "What a bunch," he said feelingly. "Now look here, Mac," he went on, "I personally don't believe that you knew anything about Tommy's being seven, but we've got to be realistic about this. If this leaks out and ends up in the newspaper, you may have to go. You see the position I'm in."

"Yes, sir."

It was an awful feeling when I left Mr. Ellsworth's office to realize that this thing might not be over yet. I had expected it all to be settled one way or another at the meeting. The way things had been left meant that I'd have to be dashing to get the paper every day, waiting to see if the story had leaked and if the ax was about to fall. One of the worst things about it was that since it was so important to keep the story quiet, I wouldn't be able to talk about what was on my mind to anyone around here. I couldn't even say anything about it to Polly.

That night I called Dad to report on the meeting.

"Hang in there, Mac," he said. "That's all you can do."

"You should have seen those Willow Green coaches," I said. "I've met friendlier creatures under old rocks. In fact, come to think of it, that head coach was sort of like a slug."

"I don't see that it's particularly in their interest to spread the story," said Dad thoughtfully. "Mud like that always sticks to the sport, makes people wonder if all the participants are a bunch of crooks."

I didn't think the Willow Green coach would follow Dad's line of reasoning, and said so.

"They've got the ribbon," Dad reasoned. "They don't have anything to gain by airing their grievance."

"Sometimes when people are mad," I pointed out, "they just spout off for the heck of it."

"Well, you'll just have to wait and see," he said.

After we hung up, it occurred to me that that might be the hardest part.

Chapter Six

The next day, Monday, was the day the pool was chlorinated, so after I put the chlorine in and checked the pH reading, I was off the rest of the day. Naturally, the first thing I did when I got off was to go by the market and get a local paper. I told myself the story hadn't had time to show up in the paper yet, even if the Willow Green coach wanted it to, but I just had to see that paper. I wondered how long I should reasonably stay worried. How long would it take for the news to get so stale that nobody would be interested? And what were the chances that the story would leak, after all? I couldn't sort it all out, but I felt a heavy sense of dread.

Back at the apartment I carefully went over the whole paper from the front page to the snippets of household hints to the wedding news; then I folded it up and decided I had

better get outdoors and do something else before I went crazy worrying. Just then there was a knock on my door. In the mood I was in, I figured it must be the angel of doom, but when I opened the front door, it turned out to be only Lindsay.

"I've brought you an invitation," she said, handing over an envelope. "And I need you to help me. I'm going to have a surprise birthday party for Polly."

I was finding it a little hard to switch my thinking from doom to Polly's birthday party. "I didn't know it was Polly's birthday," I said. "What do you have in mind?"

"I want you to lure her away from the house," said Lindsay. "You just take her for a walk or something. Otherwise, she'll notice all the cars driving up at my house and will know something is up."

I thought that for me to show up out of the blue and ask Polly to go for a walk would make her more suspicious than seeing cars drive up next door, but I didn't say so, since I didn't have a better idea.

"The party is going to be Wednesday at suppertime," said Lindsay. "Mrs. MacDougal is in on it, so all you have to do is go by and get Polly. Then, in a half hour, you bring her back to my house and everybody screams, 'Surprise!' "

"Wait a minute," I said. "I think I have the after-supper shift at the pool on Wednesday. Oh, well, I guess I can get Maggie to switch with me."

"O.K." said Lindsay. "I'm counting on you. Gotta go. I got a million of these things to deliver."

I propped the invitation against my wavy living room mirror. It hit me then that the party being a birthday party, people were bound to bring presents. Most likely the swim match business would blow up in my face, and I'd be leaving

under a cloud before the party ever happened. If it didn't, though, I would need a present for Polly, and I wouldn't have another chance to get one after that day. So I put my wallet in my back pocket and bicycled in to the shops at the middle of the island.

It was a beautiful day. On Beach Boulevard, sunlight reflected off the shop windows and a faint breeze swayed the hanging baskets of petunias. Down the street a couple of blocks, where the beach began, people were walking along the boardwalk, and beyond them, on the sand, you could see a couple of distant blue-and-white beach umbrellas. It was all very pretty, and it made me feel low to think of losing it all and going back to Fairview.

It wasn't going to be easy to find Polly a present. There were a lot of dress shops on the boulevard, but I didn't need dress shops. I did find a little place marked GIFT SHOP, but it was full of the most ridiculous, useless stuff you ever saw— little china figurines, Snoopy pencils, music boxes, and joke presents, like the tiny little house-shaped piece of wood labeled *Mosquito House*. I hope I never sink to the point that I give somebody a mosquito house, but after a half hour of looking around, I began to understand the desperate state of mind in which people buy such things.

Finally, I saw the book shop. I zipped right in there and started making my way through shelves loaded down with books on losing weight, picture books on the Royal Family, and books with blank pages for people who want to write their own. At last, at the back of the store, I found the place where they keep the old-fashioned kind of books—books for people who just want to read. Right away, my eye lit on the perfect thing. *Around the World in Eighty Days*. Now there was the perfect book for Polly. I guess it was a young reader's

edition or something, because it had some very fancy pictures of Phileas Fogg in his frock coat, first in a balloon, then at the Indian suttee, and so on. It was a great book, because even if you'd already read it you would still want to have it. I had it gift-wrapped. I hoped Polly would like it.

After I got back to the apartment and put the present away, I still had the whole afternoon ahead of me, and I felt restless. I decided to stop off at the MacDougals' and see if Mrs. M. would let Polly and me take the kids to the beach. That way I'd get to see Polly, it would be fun to play with the kids, and I'd also get to run around the beach some and get the kinks out. It also crossed my mind that if I'd already asked Polly for a walk once, she'd be less suspicious when I showed up on her birthday.

When I got to the MacDougals' house, Polly was in the backyard playing with the kids. Mark and Tracy had filled a pot with sand and water and were stirring leaves into it. Brian was trying to show Polly how he could ride his Hot Wheels on just two wheels. "Mrs. MacDougal's gone grocery-shopping," Polly told me.

"Do you think she would care if we walked the kids down to the beach and played a while?" I said.

"Go! We go!" the twins started to chant. Brian came barreling over and started to tug at Polly. "I wanna take my Hot Wheels," he said. "I'm gonna ride on the beach."

"I could leave her a note," Polly said. "And we wouldn't be going far away. I'm sure it would be all right." She lowered her voice. "But the thing is, the twins are afraid of the waves."

"We can build sand castles, then," I said.

"We don't take our Hot Wheels to the beach, Brian,"

Polly said, detaching him from her shirttail. "We're going to build sand castles. Won't that be fun?"

I kept the kids subdued while Polly went in to leave a note for Mrs. M. She came out carrying a straw carryall that looked as if it held enough in it for a wagon trek west, and we set off. It was only a short walk, so even the twins could make it on foot.

When we got there, our little stretch of beach was deserted for the moment. Polly spread out the beach towel she had pulled from her big basket, and when I looked out to the horizon where the ocean turns into a plain band of green against the sky, I could feel little dribbles of peace creeping into my bloodstream. I almost felt that everything was going to turn out all right, somehow.

"Wabes!" squealed Tracy. "Wabes gonna get me!" The panic spread to Mark, and they both started clinging to Polly and wailing about the awful waves. Boy, when Polly had said the twins were afraid of the waves, she wasn't exaggerating. We were thirty yards from the nearest wavelets, and they were having fits.

Brian, ever ready to help out, grabbed Tracy's foot and said, "The waves are gonna eat you up!" Then he giggled while the twins screamed. I picked up Brian by the seat of his pants. "The waves are our friends," I said firmly. "They are going to fill the cups we make in the sand, aren't they, Brian?" The twins, who had their hands clenched over their eyes, parted their fingers and peeked through to see what was up. For the moment their wails had stopped. I walked toward the water. We went out to where the sand was wet, and I got Brian to dig some holes with me. "Come see!" I yelled back at the twins. "The waves are filling our cups."

Polly took Mark and Tracy by the hand and led them out to

where we were. They peered at the holes full of water. Then a little wavelet washed up. "The sea is tickling our toes," I said. They giggled nervously. "Sea ticka me toe," said Tracy. Before long they were digging holes and even splashing in the thin wash of water.

Brian and I built a magnificent sand castle, then I hoisted him up on my back and gave him a ride as I jogged down the beach and back. After that, all of us played ball. By then Polly figured we'd better be getting back.

"At least we've worn them out," I said.

She pushed a damp strand of hair out of her face. "I used to think that," she said, "but now I think when you take them out to play hard, they're just building up their strength and endurance while you're the one that gets tired out."

Polly had the kind of light tan that is more a faint flush than anything. It suited her, I thought, a kind of honey color. And she always looked so clean. She was a very comfortable person. Nice to be around, even when something was worrying you.

Wednesday was the day of Polly's birthday party. I got Maggie to cover for me with no trouble. I left the pool at five and went home to get spiffed up. I even tried to flatten my hair down to look neat in honor of the occasion. While I was struggling with it, looking in my wavy mirror, I decided I was beginning to show the effects of all the endless worry. No white hairs yet, and no one ever heard of a pale lifeguard, but it seemed to me I was beginning to look hollow around the eyes. A few more weeks of that, and the pool was going to have to give me compassionate leave to enter a sanatorium. It was going to be hard for me not to rain on Polly's birthday party. I wasn't even sure I could manage to look cheerful.

I showed up at the MacDougals' on the stroke of six, following Lindsay's instructions. Polly answered the door. She looked surprised to see me, naturally. It was crazy to think I'd casually drop by at suppertime and ask her to take a walk. Lindsay was an airhead to come up with an idea like that. Still, having come this far, I didn't know what to do but go on according to the plan.

"Wanna go for a walk, Polly?" I muttered, shoving my hands in my pockets.

"I can't now, Mac," she said. "We're getting ready to feed the kids."

The sounds of destruction behind her showed that dinner wasn't coming a minute too soon. Tracy was lying on the kitchen floor drumming her heels on the ground. Brian was trying to take Mark's pacifier away from him, while Mark, judging from his purple face, had decided to defend it to the death. Mrs. MacDougal, who was transporting a casserole to the table, stepped over Tracy. "You go on, Polly. I've got things under control here."

Polly looked at her with blank astonishment. Mrs. MacDougal managed a brave smile. "Think of it as my birthday present to you, Polly," she said. "Take a nice walk and don't feel like you have to hurry back." Tracy took a bite out of Brian's ankle, which changed the balance of power and allowed Mark to run off with his pacifier in hand. I quickly closed the door behind Polly, hoping we could make it out of there before any blood was spilled.

As we walked away from the house, I realized that I should have acted surprised when Mrs. M. mentioned Polly's birthday. I should have said, "What? It's your birthday?" Something along those lines. I'm not very good at pretending.

We walked silently down the beach. It wasn't very good

walking, because the tide was in and the only place out of the water was the soft sand of the dunes, where your feet sink in. "I didn't think I was going to miss home," Polly said wistfully, "but I think I'm homesick."

I wasn't surprised. Nothing like trudging along through the sand going nowhere on your birthday to get you down.

"I've already asked Mrs. MacDougal if I can go home this weekend, since I couldn't on my birthday" said Polly. "Do you think you could get off work and go, too? The bus trip wouldn't seem so long if I had somebody to talk to."

"I don't think I could get away." I could have gotten away from the pool, all right. What I couldn't get away from was the daily reading of the newspaper and the worrying.

Polly didn't say anything. I glanced surreptitiously at my watch. "I guess we should be getting back now," I said finally.

"I guess so," said Polly.

When we got back within sight of the house, I saw a head peep out of Lindsay's front door and bob back in again. In a couple more minutes, another head peeped out. Polly, her eyes glued to the ground, didn't notice a thing. Personally, I had deep doubts about surprise birthday parties. I'd kill anybody who pulled it on me—getting you all depressed thinking nobody was interested in your birthday and then scaring you into fits by jumping out from behind doors at you. We walked up to Mrs. MacDougal's door. This was Lindsay's cue to call Polly to come over to her house, but there was a bad minute or two with us standing at the door while I waited for Lindsay to make her move. Finally, she stuck her head out her door and yelled, "Hey, Polly! Mac! Come over here. I've got something I want you to see."

Polly, who seemed to have lost all interest in life, began

moving obediently toward Lindsay's house. Lindsay pulled her in the door as everybody yelled, "Happy birthday!" I was braced for it, but it startled me, anyway. Inside was the whole crowd, plus balloons and cake. Polly was smiling, but tears were running down her cheeks. No wonder. The whole thing was a strain on the old nervous system.

Polly managed to blow out all her candles in one puff. It always has seemed too bad to me that by the time you're big enough to be sure you're going to get those candles out, you're just about old enough to know that not all wishes come true.

Polly seemed to really like the book I got her. She opened it up to look at the pictures and had to be told by Lindsay to get a move on and open the other presents. I was glad she liked it. I wanted to give her something to make her really happy, something that would make her run over and kiss me and say, "Oh, Mac!" I was starting to have a lot of little fantasies like that. She didn't seem like Pearce's kid sister anymore.

Lindsay served hot dogs for supper. Lindsay really liked hot dogs. Me, I had been eating TV dinners and beach party fare long enough to have started dreaming of steaks and pot roast. Of course, if I got fired, I told myself, I could have all the pot roast I wanted. Mom would be finishing up with her job and devoting herself full time to cleaning the house and cooking meals. The idea didn't cheer me up much.

After the party I bicycled back to my apartment. *Maybe it wouldn't be so bad to get fired after all,* I thought to myself. It would certainly be better than all the suspense. I locked the bicycle under my stairs and, putting my hands in my pockets, started walking through the yard toward the water. The Epsteins, who lived in the big house, were away, and I was

keeping an eye on the house. So far, no sign of fire or burglaries. Walking out toward the water, I could see that a kid was sitting on the low sea wall. It was funny. I had been thinking that was what I would do, just sit on the sea wall and brood, but here was this little boy no older than five or six who had already beat me to it. His back had the telltale look of sadness. He heard me coming up and looked behind him. Then I realized I had been wrong when I thought the kid was no older than five or six. It was Tommy Brisbane, who, as I had reason to know, was all of seven. He gave me a weak smile. "Hiya, Mac," he said.

"Hiya, sport," I said. "What are you doing over here?"

He looked at me in surprise. "I live here," he said. He pointed out his house, and I realized that Tommy was my next-door neighbor. If it hadn't been for the high shrubbery, I would probably have seen him around before.

"What's up?" I said, sitting down beside him.

He turned his head back toward the water. "I'm going to have to quit swim team," he said. "Mom says it isn't good for me."

"That's too bad," I said.

"They made me give back my blue ribbon, too," he said sadly. "It's the first blue ribbon I ever got."

"That's because you accidentally got in the wrong age class, Tommy. You did a good job, but you were just up against the wrong kids."

"It's not my fault," he said.

I patted him on the back. "It's just one of those things, sport."

"I told Brandon I was in the wrong bunch," he said, "and he told me to keep my mouth shut and do what you said." He burst into tears.

I could feel myself freeze all over. "He said *what*?" I said.

68

"He said to keep my mouth shut and do what you said. I tried to tell him I was in the wrong group. I tried to explain to Mom and Dad that it wasn't my fault, but they say they don't want to talk about it. But it wasn't my fault, Mac! It wasn't!"

"It sure wasn't, sport," I said, hugging him a little. "I'm really sorry. Maybe you can win another blue ribbon sometime."

"But I can't be on the swim team anymore," he said.

"Maybe you could win one for something else," I said. "I won a ribbon one time in a pumpkin-carving contest."

"Maybe so," he said, snuffling hard. He began to look more cheerful. "I'm a good drawer," he said. "I was the best drawer in my class last year."

"That's terrific," I said. "What you want to do is to enter some drawing contests."

"Yeah," he said.

I did my best to cheer him up, then sent him on home. Basically, from that time on I was just counting the seconds until I could get my hands around Brandon's scraggly throat. It was as clear as day that he had set me up. I tore back to the apartment and paced the floor, thinking. Would Mr. Ellsworth believe me? Brandon was his own nephew, and Tommy's parents weren't going to let him be called as a witness. I was in a heck of a fix. But much as I would have liked to hold Brandon upside down and shake him until he told the truth, I realized that the only thing I could do was to go to Mr. Ellsworth, tell him what I knew, and hope for the best.

Chapter Seven

The next morning I was up before the alarm. All night I had dreamed of Brandon. It was funny, but here I was, seventeen years old, and I had never had a real enemy before. I'm a pretty easygoing sort of guy, and I wouldn't have figured I could be as mad at anybody as I was at Brandon.

Luckily, by the time I had bicycled to the club I had calmed down enough to think straight. Quietly, calmly, I would tell the truth. If Mr. Ellsworth didn't believe me, there was nothing I could do about it, but I figured I would just quit the job and go home. There was no way I could work with Brandon the rest of the summer with him knowing he had gotten away with his underhanded scheme. Some things are more important than money.

Mr. Ellsworth was in his office when I got there. My feet

sank to my ankles in the carpet as I went in. "Hello, Mac," he said, cheerily, wheeling around in his swivel chair. As I told my story, the cheer left his face. I felt a kind of dead calm inside. There it was—the truth—but with no witnesses and no evidence. Was he going to believe it?

Finally, when I finished, he said, "I'm afraid Brandon has a lot of growing up to do." I thought he was on the wrong track there. What Brandon needed wasn't to grow up, but to be fitted for a ball and chain, but I didn't say so. Mr. Ellsworth stood up, shook my hand, and thanked me for coming.

I left his office, and while I was walking out of the club past the photos of old golf champions and then past the potted palm at the front door, I felt really let down. Mr. Ellsworth had seemed to believe me. That was something. But what was he going to do about it? It hit me that he might not do anything at all. I remembered my dad saying that part of the job of an administrator was just to listen to people beef, to let them blow off steam and then not do anything at all. It occurred to me that maybe that was the treatment I had been getting from Mr. Ellsworth.

By a miracle of good luck, it happened that it was Maggie who was working with me on the afternoon shift at the pool that day. I was glad of that because every time I thought of that rat Brandon, I could feel the veins in my neck start to swell with rage, and if he had showed up I might have done something I'd have regretted. Even as it was, I wasn't all full of sweetness and light. That afternoon, Troy Brown, an eight-year-old known to Maggie and me as the Boy Demon, got up to his old tricks again, holding another kid's head under water. I was on him like a hawk. "That's it!" I thundered. People all over the pool looked startled. "Out of

the pool!'' I yelled. ''And I mean now!'' I must have looked like King Kong looming over him, because for once he looked petrified. In a few well-chosen words, I let him know he'd be lucky to get back in the pool by August, let alone that afternoon.

At break, when I ran into Maggie at the drink machine, she said, ''What did the Boy Demon do this time? Drown an infant? I thought you were going to kill him.''

I felt ashamed of myself then. The Boy Demon was awful all right, but after all he was only a little kid, and it wasn't him I was mad at, but Brandon. I felt a little funny explaining to Maggie what was going on, since I had been keeping the whole swim match business a secret so long. As far as I was concerned, though, the top was blowing off this whole thing, and I had passed the point where I was willing to do nothing but sit around feeling guilty for something I hadn't even done. ''It's Brandon I'm mad at,'' I said. ''I hate to sound like some second-rate Western, Maggie, but this pool isn't big enough for Brandon and me both.''

She paused in her effort to tear open her potato chip bag with her teeth and said in a hushed voice, ''What did he do?''

I could feel myself getting furious all over again. ''I don't want to go into it,'' I said abruptly. I didn't, either. Why start foaming at the mouth in public? Luckily, Maggie's attention was diverted by the approach of her boyfriend, David. She trotted off to meet him, drawn like a yo-yo to his beckoning hand. Pathetic. I spent the rest of the afternoon brooding.

That night, just before I got off work, Polly came by the pool. She seemed pale in the light of the pool floodlights, and she looked grown up and distant with her hair pulled back

sleekly and tied with a scarf. "I just came by to say goodbye," she said, "and to see if there are any messages you want me to take home or any packages you want me to bring back. I'm leaving on the morning bus."

"How long are you going to be gone?" I asked. I was missing her already and she hadn't even left. I had sure gotten used to having her around.

"Four days," she said. "I'll be back by Tuesday."

"Do you have a couple of minutes?" I said. "Maybe we could have a cup of coffee together."

The only people still in the pool were a couple of middle-aged men swimming laps. I had to stand by while they were swimming, but I didn't have to watch them every second to keep them from holding people's heads under water. Compared to the day shift, it was a cinch.

I got a couple of cups of coffee in paper cups from the vending machine, and we sat down in lawn chairs at the side of the pool. One of the middle-aged men surfaced near us and snorted like a walrus, then went under again and went on with his laps.

"Is something wrong, Mac?" Polly asked.

"I've got a problem with Brandon," I said. "I've about decided I can't work with him anymore."

"What do you mean?"

"I mean I might have to quit," I said.

Polly knew all about why I needed this job and how much I had wanted it. "That must be some problem," she said.

One of the things I liked about Polly was that she wasn't nosy. She was willing to wait until I decided to tell her something and didn't feel as if she had to drag it out of me. But I wasn't thinking so much of Polly's good points right then. I was thinking that if I quit, Brandon would have what

he wanted. He would be rid of me. So would Allen Winkle, who—with me out of the way—would have a clear field with Polly. I would be back home finishing Mom's brick walk, and Polly would be dancing the night away with Winkle and Company.

I must have been looking pretty bleak, but I didn't say anything. I wanted to tell Polly everything, but I couldn't get one word out.

Polly got up. "I'd better be getting back," she said.

"I may look mad," I said to her, managing a grin, "but it's fate I'm mad at, not you."

Polly smiled faintly. "Well, that's a relief, anyway," she said.

You know how they say it's always darkest before the dawn? Well, the night I said goodbye to Polly was the dark spot, but the day after was a perfect daisy. I checked in at the pool at eight that morning, and there was no sign of Brandon. That cheered me up right away, but I was afraid it might be another case of his coming in late. Then about eight-twenty, up ran this new kid I've never seen before, a skinny blond with big ears. He came up to me all breathless and apologized for being late. "Mr. Ellsworth only called me last night," he explained. "My bike is in the shop, and I had to get my dad to drop me off on his way to work. My name's Davey Ellis."

I looked at him blankly, unable to believe that my troubles were really over. "Is Brandon sick?" I asked cautiously.

"Oh, no," said the kid. "Didn't Mr. Ellsworth tell you? Brandon had to quit. Some kind of family problem. I'm not sure what."

I was pretty sure then that Brandon's family problem was

his uncle jumping on his case. It was a great moment. I felt like doves should come winging out of the clouds carrying a banner saying *Congratulations, Mac,* while trumpets played "Happy Days Are Here Again." Instead, I just shook Davey's hand so enthusiastically he began to blush. The only blemish on my horizon was that Polly wasn't around to share the good news. I even had a moment's fear that she was so fed up with my being in a crummy mood that she was never going to want to speak to me again. I wanted her to be back so I could show her how cheerful and considerate I could be now that I wasn't plotting Brandon's murder.

Winkle had a party that night. I went, but I left early. I went home and started reading the book Pearce had given me. It was definitely more interesting than Winkle's party, believe me.

At last Tuesday rolled around. I knew Polly must have gotten back, but she didn't show up at the pool. She and Mrs. M. had probably taken the kids to the beach. I could see I had made a definite mistake when I taught the twins not to be afraid of the waves. I liked to see Polly over at the other end of the pool day after day. I didn't want her taking the kids to the beach instead. If I had thought all that out, I would have shrieked, "The waves are going to get you!" at the twins, the way Brian had.

When break time came, I had to go over and pull Maggie off her perch. "Didn't you hear me call break, Maggie?" I said. "You in a trance or something?" She climbed listlessly down her ladder and meekly followed me to the soft drink machine.

"David's gone to visit his grandparents in California," she told me, "for *two weeks.*" She made two weeks without David sound like a lifetime without nourishment.

I flipped open the tab on my orange drink. "Look, Maggie," I said. "Take my advice. It's a good thing for David to be away for a while. You can do some things by yourself. Play a little tennis. Take up a hobby or something."

"I don't want a hobby," she said. "I want David."

"You can't be hanging around his neck the rest of your life," I said, exasperated.

Maggie looked anxious. "Do you think he's tired of me being around so much? Did he say something to you, Mac?"

"For Pete's sake, Maggie," I said. "No, he did not speak to me, and who cares what he thinks, anyway? We're talking about you. You need to do some things by yourself for a change or you're going to forget how."

That's the stuff to give the troops, I thought a few minutes later, as I settled back on my perch full of orange drink and potato chips. Once I had cleared Brandon from the scene, I felt like I was brimming over with power. I could fix anything.

But remembering my strong words to Maggie, I did feel a little sheepish that night when the first thing I did was call Polly. Not that it was at all the same thing as with Maggie and David, but I had missed Polly and that was the truth. I waited until nine, when I was sure the kids would have been put to bed, then I dialed the MacDougals' number.

It rang four or five times, then Polly answered, but I almost didn't recognize her voice at first. "Polly?" I said. "This is Mac."

"Oh, Mac," she said breathlessly, "I can't talk now. Something is wrong with Brian." And with a little sob, she hung up on me.

It was really kind of scary. What could have happened to

Brian? I didn't sit around trying to guess. I ran out, hopped on my bike, and tore off toward the MacDougals'. After all, I had taken the first-aid course and could do CPR, and Polly sounded like she needed help.

I broke all records getting to the MacDougals'. When I banged on the door, I got no answer, so I just snapped the screen out of the front window and climbed in. "Polly?" I called.

She appeared at the top of the stairs. "Oh, Mac," she wailed. "I wish the MacDougals were here."

I bounded up the steps and followed her into Brian's room.

"He's fallen asleep," she said, "but he's still so hot."

The light from the hall shone in on his bed. I could tell he was sick. His skin looked bleached out but his cheeks were flushed, and his hair was damp where it fell on his forehead. He gave a little cough. "Maybe he's just coming down with a cold," I said. "Sometimes kids do get a fever when they're catching cold."

"He doesn't act like he's got a cold," said Polly.

"He's probably O.K.," I said.

We stood out in the hall to talk.

"Oh, I wish the MacDougals were here," said Polly. "I mean, you're probably right, but when he was awake he seemed so sick. I wish they were here."

"Didn't they leave you a number where they could be reached?"

"Yes, but I called the restaurant where they said they were going, and the woman in charge told me they weren't there."

We sat on the stairs where we could hear if Brian woke up. "If they just had a regular doctor here," Polly fretted, "I'd call him."

She was so upset I wanted to take her in my arms and

comfort her, but instead I said, "Look, I'll go find them. Most of the restaurants are right together on the waterfront near Beach Boulevard. I ought to be able to ride along there and find their car."

Polly's face tilted up toward me hopefully. "Do you think so? Oh, but what if they've finished dinner and gone home with friends to have coffee or something?"

I touched the tip of her nose gently. "I can give it a try anyway," I said.

As I left, I locked the front window and snapped the screen back in place. Then I biked toward town. It was funny, but it wasn't until that night at the MacDougals' that I realized how much I cared about Polly. I had had a lot on my mind, of course, thanks to Brandon the Beast, and then I had thought of Polly as Pearce's little sister for so long that it was natural that my mind needed some time to switch gears to her being a girl. That night, though, all that stuff in the past faded. As I rode along, my bike light shining a beam ahead of me, a stiff breeze was blowing in from the east, but I felt warm all over.

The western end of Beach Boulevard was full of cars, but there was no sign of the MacDougals' van. I wished I had asked Polly which car they had taken. Mrs. M. kept the van at the beach to get around in, and Mr. MacDougal drove the car when he came over. I couldn't remember exactly what the car looked like, but I was counting on recognizing it if I saw it. I began riding along the parking lots of restaurants along the beachfront. Finally, behind Solly's Seafood, I saw a green Mercury with the familiar bumper sticker: *If God isn't a tarheel, why is the sky Carolina blue?* I peered into the back window and saw two pacifiers lying on the backseat. It seemed like conclusive identification.

I went into Solly's Seafood and went poking around from

room to room, peering under fishnets, behind potted plants, and into booths, feeling like an absolute idiot, until suddenly I saw the MacDougals at a big table with several other couples. Before I even got close enough to speak to them, Mrs. MacDougal saw me and rose from her seat all white in the face as if I were a ghost. I guess I didn't look dressed for dining out, and she guessed something was wrong. "What's happened, Mac?" she said in this weird voice. Mr. MacDougal sprang up, too.

"Brian's just got a bit of a fever," I said quickly, seeing right away that she imagined the whole house had been swept away by a tidal wave and that only I had lived to tell the tale.

"I knew we shouldn't have come," gibbered Mrs. MacDougal. "Why didn't Polly phone? Oh, dear, we forgot to call with the number when we got here." She had gathered her purse and was being steered by Mr. M. toward the door, while all their friends made chirruping noises of sympathy. At least Mr. MacDougal wasn't falling apart, I thought with relief. But as I followed them out to the car, he turned to me and said in a low voice, "Does Brian really just have a fever, Mac? You can tell me the truth."

"That's really all there is to it," I said. "I promise. But Polly said she'd feel better if you were at home, so I came to get you."

"I'm glad you did," he said in this shattered voice. They jumped in the car and rounded the corner like a police car in a movie chase, their red taillights cutting through the darkness.

Boy, I thought, *I hope I hold together better than that when I become a parent*. My main wish was that Brian would turn out to be sick enough for them not to be mad at me for

spoiling their evening but not sick enough to be really sick. Well, at any rate, they should be home in two minutes at the rate they were going, and I knew Polly would be really glad to see them. That was the main thing.

Chapter Eight

Brian turned out to have pneumonia. He wasn't too sick, but the doctor pumped him full of antibiotics and ordered him to keep quiet for a week. He must have felt pretty bad, because I heard from Polly that he really did keep quiet. Since Polly couldn't drive, she ended up staying in with Brian a lot that week while Mrs. M. took the twins out. That week I began to have more and more sympathy with Maggie's point of view. It wasn't that I couldn't have fun without Polly, but I sure could have more fun if she were around. When Brian finally was allowed out of bed, it was a great day for all of us.

It wasn't so much that I saw more of Polly after that as it was that we were closer. It was no secret by then that we were important to each other. Winkle saw which way the wind was blowing and started making up to Mona. You could

see him at any of the parties looking soulfully into her eyes and blowing her hair out of his face. As for Polly and me, I have to admit it wasn't all smooth sailing. I mean, I don't usually wait until the sixth date to kiss a girl good night, for Pete's sake. The thing is, I had this terrible problem. Whenever I would be lying on the beach feeling like stroking Polly's honey-colored shoulder, I'd have an uneasy sensation that any minute Pearce was going to come striding out from behind the sand dunes. I had known Pearce long enough to have a good idea how he would feel about my going out with his baby sister.

I could see the irony of it all. A lot of the things I liked best about Polly (besides her looks) were things she and Pearce had in common. For instance, I liked the way she was quick on the uptake and interested in lots of things. And I liked the way she was a good friend. It was natural, when you thought about it, that your best friend and your girlfriend might come from the same family. But it was a heck of a disadvantage, too, and it took me quite a while before I could kick this hallucination that Pearce was following us everywhere. In spite of that, though, I was really happy. One thing about dating girls like Nancy Jane, you really learn to appreciate it when a girl like Polly comes your way.

A couple of weeks before school was supposed to start, Pearce called and said he was back from Colorado and wanted to come spend the weekend out at Silver Beach. I hadn't seen him for months, and I thought it sounded great. One thing I was looking forward to was telling him all about my problem with Brandon the Beast. I never had felt free to spout off about it to the kids around Silver Beach, figuring it would be better to let sleeping dogs lie, but I knew I was

going to love getting it off my chest when Pearce showed up. The only drawback to his coming was that I wasn't looking forward to breaking it to him that Polly and I were going together. Of course, he was going to have to know sometime, but I wasn't real keen to begin explaining. I could tell Polly wasn't overjoyed at the news he was on the way, either. Maybe she was thinking the same thing.

Pearce showed up Friday night. He unloaded his sleeping bag out of the back of the car, and I carried his duffel bag up the stairs. "How was Colorado?" I asked.

"Wild," he said. "The greatest." When we got upstairs, he tossed his sleeping bag on the floor and threw himself on the bed. He looked in great condition, as if he had been working out on an army obstacle course all summer. "Have you ever tried white water rafting?" he said. "That's living." He heaved an ecstatic sigh.

It sounded good, but I wasn't envious. After all, I had had Silver Beach all summer and Polly's company. I had a fatter bank account now, too. I was thinking that when I got home I'd broach the subject with Dad of applying at Georgetown.

"Heard from Leila lately?" I asked.

"Don't ask," groaned Pearce. "While I was out climbing mountains, she took up with this guy who spends all his time hang gliding." He bent over and unzipped his duffel bag. "He'll probably kill himself," he said with relish. He threw me a packet of photographs taken during the summer. They mostly consisted of a big mountain and a little Pearce, but one or two had a nice-looking girl with a backpack. It looked like Pearce's summer hadn't been exactly lonely.

"I thought we'd take in a movie after supper," I said. "I told Polly we'd stop by and pick her up."

"Hey, you didn't have to do that," Pearce protested.

"Polly's not going to expect to trail around after us all weekend. I'll go over and see her some other time."

"I've already asked her," I hedged.

I could tell I was facing one uncomfortable evening, and that's exactly what it turned out to be. Nothing much happened that night, really. I put my arm around Polly once or twice, and we held hands in the movie. That was all. But Pearce had this way of giving you the sensation you'd brought your great-aunt Miranda along on a heavy date. After we dropped Polly off and got back to the apartment, there was no avoiding the questions any longer.

"Are you *going* with Polly?" Pearce said accusingly, as if he wasn't sure which he distrusted more, my morals or my sanity.

"Yes," I said flatly.

"Cripes," said Pearce. "Polly is just a baby. I can't believe this! I never would have figured you were the kind of guy to take advantage of some kid."

I could feel a longing coming over me to forget years of friendship and deck him. Luckily, reason won out. "I'm not taking advantage of her," I said in even tones. "I'm just going out with her."

"That's what I said," said Pearce.

"Now, look," I said, "Polly is fifteen. You remember when you dated Sherry Milhaden before you took up with Leila? Sherry was fifteen."

He looked taken aback. "Maybe so," he said. "But Sherry was very . . . mature. Polly is just a kid."

"You just haven't noticed how she's grown up, that's all. Nobody keeps being a kid forever. Everybody changes."

For somebody so quick on the uptake, Pearce was awfully slow to take that in. There was a long pause while he thought

about it. "Maybe there's something to what you say," he said, "but it's hard for me to believe that Polly is really fifteen. She seems so young."

"I think she's old enough to know her own mind," I said.

A familiar, mischievous grin spread over Pearce's face. "She really likes you, huh? Well, why not? She could do worse."

I threw a pillow at him.

In a way it was good to have Pearce around, but all the same, I was glad when he packed up and left on Monday. It was pretty clear it was going to take him a while to get used to me and Polly. I suppose I should have found that easy to understand. It had taken me a while to get used to it, too.

A week before school started, the MacDougals started packing up to leave. The summer folks were all heading home. The afternoon before Polly left, she and I took a last long walk on the beach. We walked all the way down to Dynamite Point, where the houses kind of peter out and you have a point of wooded land. As we approached, a flock of laughing gulls took off in a swirl of white wings. They wheeled over our heads, making their odd, chuckling call.

"It's been a terrific summer," Polly said.

I squeezed her close. "It's been great," I said. Then I looked out at the water and said, "But in another way, I'm not sorry it's over."

"Because this year is going to be a big year for you," said Polly. Sometimes it's like she can read my mind.

"Right," I said. "It's going to be neat being a senior."

"And you're not so worried about college anymore."

I tweaked her nose. "Wait a minute, short stuff. Wait for me to get my words out, O.K.? Right. I'll have to borrow

some money to make it, but with what I've earned this summer and what I already have saved, I figure I can plan to apply at Georgetown.''

"I'm not looking forward to the year as much as you are,'' said Polly. "It's been good being away from home, being more or less on my own.''

There's a strong independent streak in Polly. Once I knew her better, I realized that.

"Also,'' she said, "I love Pearce, but he's not always so easy to live with.''

"I know what you mean,'' I said, "but maybe he'll be a changed man. You know, he's broken up with Leila.''

"No!''

"Yep. She took up with a guy who goes hang gliding.''

Polly laughed.

"I like that!'' I said. "Laughing at your brother's broken heart! Not very nice.'' I chased her down the beach, but since she was still laughing so hard, I caught her easily and then I kissed her. In my book, it had really been a great summer.

I had to hang around another week after Polly and the MacDougals left, because my job wasn't over until just before school started. It was a fairly boring week. Not too many of the gang were still around. And I began to worry about getting everything together for school. Finally, Dad came to pick me up about lunchtime on Labor Day. I had everything packed and ready to go. It seemed weird to be carrying my stuff out to the car, leaving the apartment empty. I took a last look out the kitchen window before we locked up. A lot of things had changed since the night I came, but

the scenery out the window was still the same. It even looked like the same sailboat moored out there.

"Have you got everything?" asked Dad.

"Yep."

"Are you sure? Have you looked under the bed?"

"Sure."

We locked up and put the key under the mat, Dad shaking his head the whole while at the sloppiness of the security.

"Look at it this way, Dad," I said. "If anyone did get into the apartment, would they find anything they wanted to take?"

He smiled. "Yes, well, I see what you mean."

We piled into the car. "Did Mom pick me up some new socks like I told her to?" I said. "Maybe it was the way I washed them or something, but I really need socks."

"I don't know if she's got around to that or not," said Dad. "She's been awfully busy."

I like that, I thought. *You leave home for a couple of months, and they forget you exist.* How much trouble could it be to pick up socks for a person?

On the way home, I talked to Dad about where I wanted to go to college and why. "I know the last time we talked about it I said it wouldn't break my heart if I had to go to State," I said, "but that wasn't exactly the truth. I really want to go to Georgetown more than anything. I know that even with the summer job I don't have enough saved to make up the difference between the costs of State and Georgetown, but I've been thinking I might get a job after school this year. I could give up football and get a job at a hamburger place or something. It's a lot easier to get a job in the fall than in the summer."

"I don't want you to have to do that," said Dad.

"Then I expect I could borrow the rest of the money," I said. "I figure if I can just work my tail off the first year, I might have a chance at an academic scholarship. And there's also a chance that by then Mom may have got her job back. You know she said her department had applied for a grant."

"I can tell you've given a lot of thought to this, Mac," said Dad, "but why don't we wait until we get home to talk about it? I know your mother will want to hear about your plans."

It seemed to me that Dad was being more than usually uncooperative. I hoped he hadn't got some idea that I should go to State for my own good or something. When we finally did get home, there was no sign of Mom. I started hoisting stuff out of the trunk and carrying it inside. It was going to be really great to have someone doing my laundry and cooking for a change. "When is Mom going to get home?" I said. I was a little hurt that she hadn't bothered to be in when we got home.

"She's had to go out on a job," said Dad. "I don't know when she'll be back."

"Out on a job?" I said. "Has Mom got a new job?" It sounded very peculiar to me. Social workers aren't usually called out on emergencies on Labor Day.

"I'm sure she'll want to tell you about it herself," said Dad.

Just then Mom came driving up in her little Mazda. She jumped out of the car and ran over to hug me. This was some trick, because she was wearing four-inch high heels in which you would think she could hardly walk. It began to seep into my mind that this was not her social worker outfit, which tended to be comfortable and nondescript. She was turned out in a suit, and her hair looked sort of more swirly than usual.

"How do you like the new me?" she laughed, noticing my

stare. "This is my dress-for-success outfit." She opened the carryall at her feet and pulled out some rubber boots and a blue denim coverall. She slipped off her high heels and stepped into the coverall. It had sleeves, very baggy pants, and it zipped up the front—it really did cover all. "This is my climbing-under-the-house outfit," she explained happily "Of course, I have a cap to cover my hair." She pulled out something that looked like a shower cap. It certainly made for a contrast to the dress-for-success outfit, you had to say that.

"What are you doing?" I said. "I mean, what is this new job of yours?"

"I'm an insurance adjuster," she said proudly. "When someone puts in a claim for damage, I go around and decide whether it's the type of damage covered by the policy and estimate how much it will cost to have it fixed."

It sounded perfectly respectable, but I just couldn't imagine Mom doing it.

"It pays much better than social work," said Mom. "In fact, it looks like I'll be earning enough so that we'll be able to send you to Georgetown with no trouble."

"I knew your mother would want to tell you herself," said Dad.

He sat down on the brick front steps. Dad is big enough that he has to give some thought to where he can sit down. It hit me that he's big in other ways, too. It didn't seem to make him feel bad to give Mom her moment of glory, to let her say that she'd be making it possible for me to go to school where I wanted. Dad could maybe stand to lose some pounds, but I figured I could do worse than to turn out like him. It was really good to be home.

* * *

That night I called Polly. Pearce answered the phone, and I asked him to get Polly for me.

"Polly? You called up to talk to Polly?" said Pearce. "Man, here I am your best friend, and you ask to speak to Polly?"

I hoped I wasn't going to have to go through this every time I called. The phone clattered to the floor, then Polly came on, sounding harassed.

"Don't mind Pearce," she said. "He's just being funny."

"I thought you said Pearce never answered the telephone," I said.

"That was before," she said. "Now Pearce is a reformed character. I think we're supposed to realize that climbing mountains has purified his soul and that he'll need to go climb mountains every summer."

I grinned. "Well, like I was saying to Pearce, everybody changes." I told her about Mom's new job.

"That's fantastic!" said Polly warmly. "You're home free now, aren't you?"

"Looks like it," I said. "When can I see you?"

Polly said her parents wouldn't think much of her going out on a school night.

"Consider yourself booked for Friday night, then," I said. "Meanwhile, I'll be in touch."

"Oh, Mac," she said. "I think I've missed you even just since I've been home."

"Of course," I said. "And you're not supposed to sound surprised about that. It's not polite. Hey, what was that?"

"I was blowing you a kiss," said Polly.

I grinned. I could tell it was going to be a great year.

To read Polly's side of this story, flip this book over and begin reading on page 1.